For Mags

Greetings from Nerja

Happy reading!

from the author

Best wishes

David

May 2022

David Stuart Robinson

Islet of Broken Dreams

David Stuart Robinson

David Stuart Robinson

Islet of Broken Dreams

Copyright (C) 2020 David Stuart Robinson
Layout Copyright (C) 2020 David Stuart Robinson
Published 2020 by David Stuart Robinson
Paperback design by David Stuart Robinson
ISBN: 9798 6575 08505
Cover art by David Stuart Robinson

First published 2020 by David Stuart Robinson
All rights reserved

This book is a work of fiction. Names, characters, places and incidents are the product of the author's imagination or are used fictitiously. Any resemblance to actual events, locales, or persons, living or dead, is purely coincidental. All rights reserved. No part of this book may be reproduced or transmitted in any form or by any means, electronic or mechanical, including photocopying, recording or by any information storage and retrieval system, without the author's permission.

Islet of Broken Dreams

David Stuart Robinson

To all the Alexandrias of this world

David Stuart Robinson

Was it not better, sometimes in life, simply to accept the good things on offer, to be simply grateful for them, even to celebrate them, without racking one's brains about the whys and the wherefores? Was that not truly the root of the problem with modern western man? And modern western woman?

Abominable Sin
Andy Lucerne

David Stuart Robinson

Chapter One

It seemed a strange fiftieth birthday present.

Nor could it exactly be a surprise, not when it came from the birthday girl herself. Nor did it seem to be particularly a matter for celebration. Sure, in a sense it marked the end of a working life, working at the behest of others. It meant change, which could be exciting. But probably more effort would be required, not less, more energy.

Plus, inevitably there were doubts. It represented a step into the unknown. Nothing was certain. But more than anything, the thought which would not leave her, however much she tried, however much she went through the acrobatics of the mind - this was not the realisation of a dream. The stark truth was that it was the abandonment of one, more like of many.

It was not so much that she had heard it myriad times from the lips of others, more that she had heard it whispered many times from her own - 'You were born out of your time, Alexandria!'

She had thought it enough to be certain about it. It always seemed to be the explanation after any experience, good or bad. Many had appeared to start well but finished badly. And then would come the verdict, the same old one.

Inevitably, the implication was that she had been born too late, that she was old-fashioned, that her values and aspirations belonged more to a previous era, one long disappeared. But that explanation always seemed to be far too easy. In fact, almost one of the problems had been that she had grown increasingly mistrustful of over-simple explanations.

On reflection, most turned out indeed to be erroneous. It paid to look further, to look deeper. It certainly paid to challenge conventional wisdom, fixed ideas, contemporary thought. Yes, sometimes the solution or the truth was delightfully simple but also a little hidden.

One often had to delve to find it. But her experience also confirmed that the search was always worthwhile. Hard thought was not as painful as its reputation would have us believe. It could even be fun. And it was always rewarding if it produced another piece in the jigsaw, the one labelled 'Understanding of Life'.

No, even after all these years she would not take this one at face value either. It was more complex, more deserving of a more multifaceted explanation, one more mature, wiser, above all one which accorded with her own feelings. Explanations only rang true, felt real, when thought and feeling could marry in close harmony. No, she had to look further.

In fact, it came like a new dawning - No, she was not born too late. Nor could it simply be said the opposite - that she was born too early. Yet there was some truth in that too somehow.

She certainly did not feel classically old-fashioned. That seemed a misnomer, not doing her justice. No, the only form of words which came her way were strange but different - 'I don't feel behind. I feel ahead. In fact, the truth is that in some ways I'm light years ahead!'

It did not make it any easier.

It did not relieve the isolation. Yes, a beam of illumination was always welcome. It was always a good feeling to have better understanding. But if the essential situation stayed the same, the relief could be brief. The solution remained stubbornly elusive. The satisfaction soon felt hollow again. So the plan still had to go ahead.

Was it worse, even? - To know? To have that clarity? One understood the situation better but one was still helpless to do anything about it. One thing which was certain, almost the first lesson learned, was that one could not change the world, which usually meant that one could not change human nature.

Even when human nature appeared to improve, it only flattered to deceive. The improvement was only illusory. It merely shifted sideways. It merely swapped old prejudices for new ones.

Any new apparent tolerance was often more than outweighed by even greater intolerance. All that seemed to be increasing unopposed was cynicism, which was more or less where she came in.

Yes, it was finally the moment to call time.

It had been building up for years. The writing had long been on the wall, just getting bigger, till in the end the wall almost seemed to be shouting at her, till in the end it was deafening and her eardrums could resist it no longer. 'Yes, stop the world! I want to get off!'

It was an old-fashioned phrase, dating from way back in the last century. Someone had even written a musical show with such a title, when perhaps in the post-war period the lunacy first started to appear. But if one thought about it, that lunacy had nothing on that of the present day, which seemed in comparison to be out of control.

So how many people nowadays either voiced the words or at least felt the sentiment? Probably relatively few. The media was doing too good a job. How many thought for themselves any more? More, how much larger was the majority which just accepted the spoon-fed views of the resigned, the passive, the compliant? Consumerism occupied their hearts and minds much more fully than real curiosity, independent thought, idealism.

Surely, idealism, along with romanticism, was dead. They had been buried long before and the earth covering them had only been hardened by millions treading them underfoot. The buffalo and the Red Indian of North America had in the space of a short century been replaced by another stampede, even more irresistible, one which had arguably spread worldwide, its tentacles everywhere. If one looked around, really looked with searching perceptive eyes, one could see many other 'RIP's.

Chapter Two

She refused to have an early retirement presentation at work.

When she asked herself, she did not want one. It would only be to please others, as usual. And was that not the point, especially now, on this very day? - That she was saying goodbye to the world of pleasing others? She had had a bellyful of it, all her life. Was that not a good part of the why of today? Of her reasoning? Her motivation?

The world, in all its spheres, insisted on one's not just following its rules but also its convention, its norms. Fail to follow and you were labelled at the least a spoilsport. Maybe that was in truth how she was perceived today - by work colleagues, who doubled as friends, who at least acted out the role.

So instead, she invited a few of them for an after-work drink in the nearest bar. It was something, a gesture, a concession. In a sense it seemed a small price to pay, just the last on a long list dating back years.

What exactly was the bargain?

Even she seemed unsure. There seemed to be so many unfathomables. Certainly she was not in a position to draw up any sort of balance sheet. Yes, she was freeing herself - from work, from the discipline of its regularity, also from most of the income from it. From now on, in a sense, she would be answerable to no-one. The word 'boss' she could, if she wished, erase from her vocabulary.

But she was also saying goodbye to things like security, like predictability. Viewed from the outside, her little life had appeared so orderly. The mistake had been, on the part of just about everyone, to assume that the inside of her head was the same, when in fact it had been the complete opposite.

Now it was that inside mind which was finally going to flip the coin over. The only trouble was that she had no idea, no, not even she, what the reverse looked like. That was what she was now expecting to find out in the next weeks and months. No doubt there would be much of the unexpected, many surprises, maybe even nasty ones. If she had in a sense been able to control things in the past, that was the last thing that she would be able to do from now on.

Again it was all part of the deal. No-one was forcing her. But she had taken her decision and she was determined that, come what may, she would always stick to her maxim, one taken from the song of one of her few heroines from the past - 'No regrets!'

The happy state of the housing market - for sellers, not buyers - meant that she had the luxury of choosing the potential purchaser.

She engaged an agent but insisted on being present at all the viewings. The visitors were not aware of it but while they were inspecting the house as a potential future home, they were at the same time being interviewed.

In the end she accepted not the highest bid but the one from the youngest couple. They were clearly the ones who were struggling the most to scrape together the deposit, plus she had not failed to see a prominent anatomical bump which indicated that their days as a mere twosome were numbered.

"For an extra thousand you can have all the contents, cutlery and all!"

Even the couple realised that those contents were worth at least five times that amount. The truth was nearer ten times as much. But all parties were content. The deal also enabled her to dictate certain terms, in particular the precise timing.

"Monday, 1st April! Not a week before! Not one day later!"

A few eyebrows were raised. The odd half-smirk was to be seen.

"No, I'm not joking. This is no April Fool's Day prank."

No dissenting voices. Instructions would be duly dispatched to solicitors, building societies, banks and estate agents. No slip-ups!

Everyone understood.

"I hope," she could not help adding with a small smile, "that you enjoy my taste in literature."

So she had all weekend to pack a 50 litre rucksack.

So she had all weekend to pack a 50 litre rucksack which had been packed for weeks, first in her head, second in reality. What a contrast! What a narrowing! What a down-sizing! She was exchanging a houseful, selling it for a paltry £1,000, to slim down to a backpack, which when full would weigh a mere 25% of her slender frame.

Was she mad? Most would not even bother to ask the question but would skip over it and go straight to the emphatic answer. It was one reason why she had had to keep it all so secret.

She did not like being vague. It did not come naturally to be evasive. It came even less naturally to string them all a pack of half-truths, more grey than white lies. Nor was it to preserve her own sanity, not in our own eyes at least, just to preserve it in the eyes of others. Anything for a quiet life!

Everything else was booked. Nothing was left to chance. She could even largely take the whole weekend off, indulge herself, celebrate wildly, get dead drunk, still with time to get over the hangover and sober up by 9 o'clock on the Monday morning.

Somehow the idea did not appeal. No, what little celebration there was to be was already done, with half a dozen work colleagues, now ex-work colleagues.

In any case, in keeping, should this not be more like a wake? Was it not more like some sort of interment? A burial? A good-bye? It did feel more like one. In mood the whole weekend was just like that - a quiet mourning, like a lone bereaved, where friends and family, uncomfortable, dared not call round.

Chapter Three

When doing the planning, months before, she thought it a wise move to leave a final blank weekend, in case there were still some loose ends to tie up.

In the event there were none. Her planning and the execution were almost too good. Everything had gone like clockwork. She was too efficient by half. She always had been. Maybe that was her trouble.

But no, seriously, maybe that was her trouble.

Maybe it was off-putting. It was curious in life - what made some people more popular than others. One could be surprised until eventually, almost through bitter experience, one stopped being surprised and just accepted the world, meaning human nature, as it was.

One might start out, young, with one's naïve beliefs. Unless there were elements in one's upbringing to discourage one, one might grow up believing in good, thinking that it was important to be kind, considerate, punctual, orderly, conscientious, all those things.

But then at some point - it could be sooner or it could be later - one found oneself having to revise one's thinking, in a word most likely throw it all in the bin. Because when one looked around, it was not those types of people who were popular, who were successful. It was almost the opposite.

Who were the popular ones? Who were the ones who enjoyed success, in both their personal and professional lives? It was the others - the ones who did not give a fig about anyone else, the unreliable, irresponsible ones who seemed the opposite of kind. Those were the ones to whom everyone gravitated, who were courted in all spheres. That was the way of the world and the sooner one got used to it and accepted it, the better.

The problem was that Alexandria had not.

It was not that she was unobservant or stupid. She saw what was happening all right. It was just that she could not quite bring herself to accept it, not even if the non-acceptance were to her own detriment.

Her vision was different. Okay, events, the proofs to be seen, might not back it up, might appear even to destroy it. But somehow she could not quite bring herself to throw it in that bin. Nor could she, hand on heart, add - 'Not yet'. If she had her hand on her heart, then she could only add - 'Not ever!'

That in a nutshell was what this was all about, this fiftieth birthday present.

It was not throwing in the towel really, not the big one. It was not saying - 'Okay, world, you win! Finally I agree to go down your cynical path. Thus I will finally get my due.'

No, but it was a kind of withdrawal from the ring nevertheless, from the contest, throwing in the smaller towel. It was an admission that, no matter how long the bout went on for, it was apparent now, over halfway through, that she could not win, that she could never win. The odds were too stacked against her.

Maybe the weighing machines had been fiddled with or something. Maybe she had been given the wrong gloves, or a fake gumshield. But whatever it was, the referee or the panel of judges seemed to have made up their minds already and it would not be her arm, her fist, that they would at the end be raising in that gesture of victory.

So better to leave the ring now with a bloody nose rather than later with cracked ribs or a broken jaw. No, in the course of that last year, her fiftieth, the alarm bells had been ringing and all the old feelings had been nagging away inside her.

Her time was up. Her career was over. She would not go on to become world champion. She would not go on to be any sort of champion. In fact, the reality was that she would not win, in truth had never won, a single bout.

Time to retire. Better than that - time to retire from everything!

During a career stretching over twenty-five years she had never lost a client.

It was a record, unheard of, not only within her own particular firm of accountants but within the local professional circles. At the annual regional dinner someone was always bound to raise the subject, half in jest.

Alexandria was never quite sure whether she welcomed the mention or indeed the reputation. In a sense it almost pigeonholed her, as some kind of freak. She got too used to the condescending smiles, to those looks of complete indifference from all the male colleagues, almost looks of pity from the fewer female ones present.

9 o'clock on Monday morning saw her standing outside the door to the solicitors' office, ringing the bell.

Not long afterwards, in fact within minutes, all the other parties arrived. These matters always felt a little fraught, even right up to the last day, but in this case it did not look as if there were going to be any last-minute hitches. All the paperwork was done. All funds were in place. Nobody had had a last minute change of heart. On the contrary, it seemed that all parties present were enthusiastic to proceed.

In less than an hour it was all done. Multiple signatures had been written on multiple documents. The ink was dry. Some even permitted themselves a small smile. Lives were changing, more than one. There was no going back now. All that remained was for the vendor and the two purchasers to repair to the property, the subject of the sale, in order to hand over the last essentials - the keys.

"I just have my rucksack to pick up, then it's all yours."

"We're packed up too. We'll go back and bring our things over later this morning."

It was all done with such delightful simplicity. Where was all the stress? With this transaction it seemed to be notable for its absence.

Half an hour later and the keys had changed hands. Her rucksack on her back, she was about to go through another door, her own, her own front door, in an outwardly direction and for the last time, the last time ever. In truth it was now her former front door. She was no longer the owner. In fact, she no longer had a UK address.

'Stepping outside, she was free!'

The trouble was, the song not quite somehow ringing true, that she was not some stifled but daring teenager, nor did she have anyone waiting for her, not even a man from the motor trade. No, she was on her own now, now more than ever. Yes, stepping outside, she was free indeed. Free but alone.

Chapter Four

There was something about rail travel.

Especially if you did not have anything to read. Of course, she could have bought half a dozen books at the station. But she had promised herself to travel light and, if anything, leave behind the trappings of her former life.

In any case, she was in no mood for reading and doubted if on the shelves of a railway station bookshop she would find anything remotely interesting, in particular relevant to where she was going, not just geographically but also psychologically, emotionally.

So on a train, with a window seat, almost inevitably her eyes were drawn to the passing scenery. At first it was urban and ugly. Later it was rural and beautiful. And there was something somehow about watching the passing countryside whizz by. It was almost like watching her life whizz by. Maybe after all she would not have to wait until the last few seconds of her life to see the rerun. She could see the show now.

And so it seemed. As the countryside flew by at 100 kph, so her past life seemed to be retreating. Each few miles seemed to account for each year. Soon ten were gone. Then before long another ten. Before journey's end all fifty would be accounted for. Was it appropriate that the early morning sun had given way to light cloud, then to darker cloud, then to a light drizzle?

What had been remarkable during those years?

Was she going to have to reply? - 'Not so very much!' Maybe in truth that would be most people's reply. But somehow, she could just not get away from the nagging feeling that in her case it really was not so very much, but less.

As she looked out of the window at the passing countryside, a wry smile passed across her features. Less. Why was it a word which always seemed to accompany her? Why did it always appear that she had less? Of everything?

But what made it even more ironic now was that, where she was going, she would have even less than in the past. Not only that but it was deliberate, calculated. In a sense she was going for the 'lesser' option. It was her choice, no-one else's. Whatever she had had in the past, now she was heading for even less.

The airport drew another wry smile from her lips.

How fitting it should be - that a huge international airport should represent her last foothold in her old country. Surely there was nothing more representative, more symbolic, like the apotheosis of 21st-century western civilisation.

Were a spacecraft from Mars to happen to land at an international airport, then there would be no need to show the occupants anywhere else. They would get it in one, in ten seconds flat. In another ten seconds they would know what Homo Sapiens was about, not so much where his roots lay but certainly his ambitions. As a snapshot it would be perfect, something to take back to Mars with, to show the family, for they would be unlikely to stay, any more than Alexandria.

Her wait was mercifully short, the minimum.

That way she seemed to keep moving, so that there was little time to dwell on things, to reflect, whether about international airports or uneventful lives which were being left behind.

Once again she had a window seat. In a sense there was less to look at, mainly just blue sky. One could look down but it meant craning one's neck and then maybe only to see the tops of fluffy clouds, not so interesting as the wet English countryside.

No, she had not even allowed herself the luxury of a guidebook.

A so-called quality newspaper would have to serve to occupy her grey matter for a while. Even there she turned straight to the back, to the sports pages. Anything but politics! Was that not after all part of what she was escaping from? Just now she would not mind if she never saw another politician in her whole life. In truth, just now, politicians were not the only people, or things, which she would not mind never ever seeing again in the her whole life.

At least the football league title was brewing up nicely for the last month and a half of the season, even if the chances of her being able to keep track of it after today were scant. For that reason she decided, on leaving the aircraft, to take the back pages with her, crosswords and all. It was not nostalgia, not yet. But perhaps she would have to admit to being, just a little bit, a sentimental old fool.

Alexandria was not unused to travelling.

In a way it had always been the one little luxury which she had permitted herself. She had spent many reasonably happy holidays touring France, which somehow had led to her keeping up a decent working knowledge of the language.

That had even influenced her with other choices of destination. Twice - inevitably against the advice of friends and colleagues - she had ventured into North Africa, in particular to Morocco. She had even gone further south, out into the Indian Ocean to the large island of Madagascar.

But within her wildest dreams she would never have imagined that knowledge of a western European language, one spoken by a people barely 35 kms across the water from the British Isles, would ever come back to serve her on the other side of the world, as near as dammit to the Antipodes in fact, in the midst of the biggest ocean in the world, even in the southern hemisphere.

Plus, most times not through choice, she was not unused to travelling alone. There had been little question of travelling together as part of a conventional couple. And whilst it was common enough for two women to travel together, for a woman to go on holiday with a girlfriend, with her it had rarely happened.

There just seemed to be no-one suitable. Or if a name did come into the frame, it soon became apparent that their tastes were too different, even their mode of travel. Most women, particularly as they got a bit older, seemed to need that element of luxury, or security, particularly on holiday. They always wanted to rely on couriers or guides, as if abroad they needed protection.

Alexandria was the opposite. So what was the hope of making a compatible voyage? On holiday two people spent more time together than did a married couple. That was another matter, not completely irrelevant. Best not go there. The trouble was that two and two added up to make four.

So solo it was.

So solo it was, it seemed, in practically anything. It also meant that this so far was not so strange. But funnily enough, it also meant that at the other end it would be different. For the first time there would be 'link' people. But it did not produce any feeling of confidence, of comfort, in her. This time she would inevitably be partly in other people's hands.

But this time there was no alternative. This time she would have to trust. It was a means to an end. That end was a regaining of that independence, and not the old one but a new one. Put it like this - this time she was really going to find out the meaning of the expression 'self-reliance'.

She did at least already know one of the intermediaries.

She had met him in the course of her first trip, the 'recky'. It was he who owned the boat, who had shown her the island. She had even met his family. They were not exactly living in the lap of luxury. The commission which he asked for seemed modest by any standards, less than what she expected.

She had been determined not to pay any sort of premium, as if for the privilege of being a foreigner. Of course, it went on all over. Just a few astute locals got rich. But she was determined not to play that game. She would turn her back first. She would walk away if necessary, even leave them to it.

If they needed to, they clearly got the message. In the end it seemed that they would just be glad to get it off their hands at any sort of price. She offered a sum which was ridiculously low, almost an insult, and it was accepted.

Thinking about it now, if owing to climate change the whole island became submerged in a matter of years, it would not represent such a great loss. She could easily start again somewhere else.

But such submersion was far from likely. She had checked it out. She had checked everything out. No, not everything was in tiptop condition but everything worked - everything! She had made sure, had made them prove it.

She might make further improvements but that was up to her. After a while it might be a case of simply needing a project. But all that would be at her discretion, something for the future. Just now, flying at 35,000 feet, with only an expanse of blue ocean below to look down upon, she had more immediate things on her mind.

Would he be there to meet her? Would everything go as smoothly as promised? Or would there be nasty surprises crawling out of the woodwork? She had done her best, done her homework, to try to ensure that none did. After that, all she could do was cross her fingers. All hers were crossed as the jet engines sped her across the sky.

Chapter Five

Suddenly, halfway through the flight, she seemed to relax.
"Fuck it!"
Yes, she did say it out loud but not such that anyone else was likely to hear. But what would her ex-colleagues think? They would be shocked.

'Alexandria swore! Whatever next? Can anyone see pigs flying?'

She ordered herself an apéritif - anis, not so heavy on the water, roughly half and half - plus red wine with the meal. Long haul flights were not so stingy when it came to measures and quantities, compared to short haul.

She soon began to feel merry. It seemed like the first time in ages. She literally could not remember the last time. It had most certainly not been at her early retirement drinks party the previous Friday.

Merry was the word, the right word. She felt merry, jolly, happy. Okay, it was only temporary, due to alcohol unusually running through her veins. But it was such a pleasant feeling, all the more so for not having been felt for such a long time. And the chances were that she could keep this nice little merry feeling topped up for the rest of the flight, all the way to Sydney. She did.

So the flight passed more swiftly and more agreeably than she had anticipated or imagined.

She had a few hours to kill now, before she boarded a connecting flight to Nouméa. She took a few drinks, even had a meal. She found some brochures and information sheets at a tourist office. There was not much about Pacific islands. There were more maps and leaflets about French Polynesia than about New Caledonia. She read those too. Most were tourist propaganda but some useful information could be gleaned between the lines. Photographs in general still did not lie.

Everywhere the problem was the same - that idyllic unspoilt little locations were discovered all too soon, especially as the century progressed, especially if those places were reasonably accessible. Often there was just one international airport hub but many of the outlying islands had small airports, if just an airstrip. Of course, no doubt it proved a lifeline for the inhabitants, even boosted local economies by encouraging tourism.

But everything was a two-sided coin. Ways of life were invaded, even changed. Money talked. No-one, it seemed, was immune to its influence. The fact of the matter was that even remote Pacific islands could now be drawn within the web of the expanding and voracious western money spider. The challenge was still to find and then reach those which, for a variety of reasons, appeared less attractive and were likely to remain so. Sheer inaccessibility often proved an effective barrier. Yes, sometimes a negative could be turned into a positive.

Alexandria found herself musing on such matters, as she waited.

She did not rack her brains, even less rage against the universe. She had accepted long before the good and the bad about the human race. Yes, greed seemed to be a stronger motivator more than kindness, when one might wish for the converse. But was not this very project proof that she accepted the situation as it was? She was not going to change it.

Having perhaps hoped for change for fifty years, she had decided that she was not going to spend the next fifty in the same hope. This was acceptance in action. Whatever fight, or resistance, that there might have been was now over. She was stepping off the stage, hanging up her costumes and shoes. She would find a way of stopping the world and stepping off. In fact, she was not far away now.

She suddenly noticed that her onward flight was boarding.

She kept half the brochures and discarded the rest. Even the next flight was relatively uninteresting. Down below was just more blue ocean. Most islands were too small to make out, The only substantial one was New Caledonia itself, the main island, Grande Terre. At least the flight was considerably shorter, less than three hours.

She was feeling good, light, as she passed through the high ceilings of La Tontouta international airport. This time she barely gave it a second glance. Were not all international airports roughly the same? - At their best when you were leaving them. At their very best when you were leaving them for some considerable time.

The man was waiting.

In fact he came straight up to her, bowed and offered to relieve her of her rucksack. She declined. She was intent on keeping as much of her independence as possible. He led her to a waiting car. Soon her rucksack was safely stowed in the boot. In a sense she could relax again.

The first time she had had to make her own way. Naturally she had chosen public transport. That was always interesting, could even be fun, but it was rarely less than complicated, especially when there were connections to be made.

At least this way she could just sit back and leave all the logistics to someone else. In theory at least, a small conveyance driven by a local should, in a fraction of the time, convey her from international airport to some small obscure port, not necessarily in less than no time but without hitch or interruption. She could sit back. She did.

It did seem in less than no time compared to the last time.

Mind you, last time, she had, as was her wont, made plenty of detours, if only out of sheer curiosity. In fact, the small obscure port had not been her original destination, had not even been on her list. It was only when, late one evening, she got chatting to some locals in some godforsaken bar, that someone suddenly started romancing about the little island some way off shore.

"It's owned by an Australian couple but they're not there any more. They were wanting to sell up but they've left already, gone off to make a new life back in the arms of civilisation, I guess, with less austerity. Well, he was Australian. I think that she was European, maybe French, I can't be more specific. From all accounts they loved it. But I guess that there comes a time when the dream fades a little, or the years catch up, or you simply change, get a different outlook. They put it on the market, saying - 'If it sells, we'll go. If it doesn't, we'll stay.' But in the end they didn't. Instead they packed their bags and halved the price. Rumour has it that they would halve it again. And maybe again!"

The conversation seemed to conclude with rather ribald alcohol-fuelled laughter, which did not displease Alexandria. She liked the rich colour of local life, even identified it as her main reason for travelling. But all the words had registered with her all right, whatever the degree of truth in them.

To put it slightly differently - by the end of the following day she was staying in a shack just outside the small obscure port on the other side of the island, having arranged to hire the following day a boat with an outdoor motor, a craft which looked alarmingly small to be taking on such a watery trip, covering the expanse to what to all intents and purposes was a desert island.

"Don't worry! It's not called the Pacific Ocean for nothing!" had said the man on the tiller.

She did not feel so reassured. She had not always lived by the maxim - 'Nothing ventured, nothing gained!' But it would appear that all this foreign air - or drink! - had conspired to make her take a chance on it now.

Only a few months later, she was now returning a second time - as the owner!

Chapter Six

"The Australian lived there for more than twenty years."

Alexandria looked at the man on the tiller. He was just looking straight ahead. It was almost as if he were just thinking aloud.

"The Frenchwoman for just over ten years. So they must have liked it. I did a bit of transporting for them in the early days but later on they had to get someone else, someone with a bigger boat and more muscle. They were bringing over heavier stuff - large fridges, a chest freezer, an old upright piano, eventually even a desalination plant. It must have been very primitive when he first moved out there. Have you ever had a shower in seawater? I can tell you that it's not great. But he must have loved the way of life enough to put up with it, even the isolation. I suppose that it was what he was seeking at that time. Maybe it's what we're all seeking some of the time. But he had the guts to actually do something about it, to turn those aspirations into reality."

She was still looking at him, taking it all in but refraining from comment.

"But as you saw on your first visit not so long ago, it's reasonably civilised now. No, it's not exactly like a five-star luxury hotel, not like some of these expensive tourist islands that are advertised now as paradise. People just go to those for a couple of weeks, maximum three or four, never longer. This is different. This is all the year round stuff. But I guess that you've thought about all that and are prepared for it."

For once he took his eyes off the water ahead and looked at her. She just nodded back. She was quite happy to let him go on.

"So in the end it cannot have been the living standards which turned them away from the idea of living out the rest of their days there. No, those were pretty good, everyone agreed. So it must have been the other thing - the isolation. He did get a few visitors, so I heard, the occasional friend, a long lost relative, plus one or two adventurers, who heard about the place from locals and whose curiosity got the better of them. These would be largely self-sufficient types. Put it like this - even if the welcome which they hoped to receive were not in the event so overwhelming, then they could look after themselves for a few days before another passing boat came to take them off."

Meanwhile Alexandria was feeling as calm as the water.

Maybe it was as if it were all too late now anyway. Even if the man on the tiller did say something displeasing, did reveal a drawback hitherto unmentioned, she would not let it daunt her, not now. She had travelled too far, not just geographically in the last few days, but psychologically and emotionally over a period.

Even there, one might question how recent it had been. Of course, as the project became more concrete, even threatening to come to fruition and sooner rather than later, she had had to let go of much, of much from her previous life. But in many ways that process had been going on for some time, for years, maybe for decades.

Who knew when it might have begun? In early adulthood? Or even earlier, during adolescence? Or even earlier still, during infancy? Still so little was known about childhood, about what thoughts and feelings we experienced back then, how much they would go on to influence our later life.

It was almost as if progress in psychology had come to a standstill. It still seemed to be very much groping in the dark. All it seemed to be able to come up was the thesis that frustrated mothers resented their kids and that knots in the stomach while commuting meant that you hated your work. Maybe it was best left there, as a kind of self-congratulatory dead-end.

No, the die was cast now. Not for the first time, against all perceived wisdom, she had now put all her eggs in one basket. If she should have the misfortune now to drop said basket, then there could be only one result - no omelette for tea! In fact, nothing for tea! Just a rumbling empty stomach!

"We don't get much rainfall here."

The man on the tiller continued his monologue.

"What we get falls mainly in what we call the hot season, December to March. But it rarely gets very hot, not like in some places, even in Europe. Nor does it ever get cold, not even at night. The only thing that you've got to watch out for weather-wise is the occasional cyclone or even typhoon. There's no particular pattern but about once every ten years or so we get hit by a big one - high winds, lasting for days, sometimes bringing heavy rain, often between February and April. The trouble is that it always comes without warning. Not even all this new technology can, it seems, give us more than the briefest of notice. And then it's all wild panic, of course, a case of battening down the hatches in double-quick time, triple if possible. Put it like this - when it does hit, whatever is not tied down, better nailed down, is not going to stay around. Come the morning or the day after, it's going to be flying halfway across the ocean."

Alexandria's expression did not change. If anything a small smile crept across her lips. Okay, she might have come for the quiet life but even she would not want it that quiet. In fact, had she not always liked a little bit of the unpredictable? How much she did like that - the unpredictable - it looked very much as if during the coming months she was going to find out.

Her eyes left the man on the tiller and followed his, looking straight ahead. No longer was there just water, just ocean, to be seen. A small island had come into view.

Chapter Seven

Alexandria had been such a happy child.

Looking back, that idyllic childhood might in the end have done her a disservice. But should one ever regret good things? Probably not.

Unusually, her parents lived with one set of grandparents, on her father's side. Alexandria had an elder sister, Jennifer. They all lived in a large house out in the country. It was a safe environment, in just about all aspects. The girls could play out without danger. They could even explore - the nearby woods and fields. They could climb hills and trees. Things were natural.

Above all, she was secure. If occasionally one of the other children at school was cruel, or at least unkind or insensitive, then there was always a shoulder to cry on at home later on. In truth she had not much tendency to cry. In further truth there was really not much to cry about.

Thus she grew up, able to express herself freely in every way. She learnt to play the piano, loved to paint the beautiful scenes outside. She was healthy. Worries were few. The summers seemed long.

So no-one warned her about the big bad world outside.

Even during adolescence, when inevitably it invaded more, she still refused to believe it. She managed to devise somehow, in her mind, a way of classifying all disappointing events - invariably being let down by friends or others - as 'exceptions'. In fact, it was one of her favourite sayings - 'The exception proves the rule.'

The trouble was that as her years advanced, as she passed through the second half of teenage, those exceptions seemed to increase, in reality multiply. It was not so much that she did not notice, more that she was reluctant to abandon a belief system which she had spent the whole of her short life building.

Having good looks and generally being of a happy disposition made her attractive.

She did not lack friends. And as the years passed, she was not short of suitors, boys, young men, who were more than ready to walk out with her, make her their girlfriend.

At first she was wary. It was not that her parents or grandparents or even her elder sister had warned her off or anything, had told her to be careful. More it came from within. She trusted her instincts and what she lacked in experience she had sort of gleaned from exposing herself to the arts, literature and the theatre, music and painting.

She was not frightened of life, more the opposite. She seemed to embrace it more fully than most. But she had been to the cinema a few times too and had not always liked what she saw there, in particular the behaviour of young people.

That behaviour and its motivation seemed to depart quite markedly from her own philosophy of life, if it could be termed such. She seemed instinctively to rebel against the shallow feelings, the cynical approach to life, this notion of using others for one's own advancement, whether in personal or professional life. After a while she stopped going and left her little band of friends to continue the cinema visits without her.

Generally speaking she seemed happy enough to knock around as just one of the crowd. If most of her girlfriends had boyfriends, it did not did not seem to bother her. Nor could she help noticing that not all of them always kept what might be called a happy disposition. All too often nowadays she was finding that it was she who was providing the shoulder to cry on. No, it was not her own direct experience, only second-hand, but she felt that she was learning not a little from the accounts being related.

At university, away from home for the first time, she could not help feeling that first flush of freedom.

She looked around and saw that it went to the heads of many.

This was not cinema now, fiction. But it looked as if many of her fellow undergraduates were desperately trying to imitate their screen idols. Put it like this - times had certainly changed. Habits and personal mores had certainly changed.

Once again she did not like all that she saw. She more or less made her mind up that she would not number among those who seemed desperate for 'experience'. In any case, she had her studies to pursue and as at school planned to take them seriously.

Chapter Eight

It was only in her third and final year that eventually she was asked out by a boy whom she did rather like.

He seemed different somehow. He too had grown up in the countryside. He seemed steadier than the others. They had interests in common. Above all, he seemed the perfect gentleman. After a while it seemed the perfect match.

Not uncommonly or unexpectedly, with time Benjamin wanted to take matters further, to deepen the relationship. He had been patient thus far, content with just a bit of slap and tickle before a prolonged goodnight kiss. No doubt too he felt that he was missing out when he knew that all his mates were overnighting at their girlfriends'.

Alexandria managed to keep him at arm's length, just. It was their last year at Uni. They needed to study hard for their final exams. She was aiming for a first in mathematics. All in good time.

Come the end of term, the end of the academic year, in fact the end of their university career, before knowing the results, she agreed to go on holiday with him.

But before even the flight was booked, she made it plain to him that she was not going to sleep with him. She insisted on separate rooms.

"But we're as good as engaged, Alex!" he protested.

" 'As good as' is not the same as actually being so. I prefer to wait until we are."

"But it's not as if you're religious even!"

"No, but nevertheless, I have my own beliefs, ideas. You must have realised by now - that I'm romantic, that I believe in love. I have feelings too, strong ones, but it's not always the right thing to gratify them, not immediately. I like to think that love comes first and that this way, it has a better chance of lasting, even for ever."

It was so out of step - not just with him but with everybody.

Practically no-one entertained such outdated notions of love any more. In fact, nowadays they sounded almost comical, as if someone were satirising a nineteenth century novel. Surely, she could not be serious. But by now Benjamin knew her well enough to know that she was. Somewhat reluctantly, when he booked the flights, he reserved two single rooms for their first night in Havana.

It was a long flight, the longest that either of them had undertaken thus far.

Nevertheless, they were both in good spirits. The exams were over. True, the world of work now awaited both of them. But before then, they had a summer of freedom to look forward to, like a last throw of youth before getting weighed down by responsibilities. A carefree holiday awaited in a new and fascinating land. During the flight she even permitted herself red wine with the meals and got a bit giggly.

Havana was confusing, to say the least.

They had to be on their guard. Maybe even one night would be enough before heading off to somewhere a little less intimidating. At the end of their stay, on their way back, no doubt having got used to this strange Caribbean country, they could always spend their last couple of nights in the capital too.

The railway station they found no less confusing. Most trains were cancelled anyway. The schedules were chalked up on a big blackboard, a whole list of entries, most the same -

'Tren Anulado - Falta de Combustible'

It seemed that the country, after the collapse of the Soviet Union, which had propped it up for three decades, was now going through something of a crisis.

They made their way to the bus station. Maybe the buses,

unlike the trains, would have some fuel to run on. There was an overnight coach leaving in the evening, heading east. Things were not exactly going to plan but at least they were together and could smile at the relative lack of order about the place, the odd way of doing things. They would spend a few days in Bayamo, maybe do a bit of hill-walking.

It was no-one's fault really.

The lady who led them from the bus station to the house naturally assumed that they were a couple. There was only one room licensed to let. Before Alexandria had the chance to say anything, Benjamin had already said it.

"Fine! We'll manage!"

But they did not. Or rather, they did not manage very well. This time he really did expect her to share the bed with him and when she point-blank refused, he just sulked all night long.

In a curious way, she could not find it within her heart to blame him. After all, it was the culture of the age. It was as if there were now an understanding throughout society. It had turned the page on such sensibilities. Okay, you could still protest, still hold out, still fight your corner. But now it was the done thing to give in eventually. 'Full marks for trying! Respect gained! But now, for heaven's sake! It will soon be the 21st century!'

The next day they parted.

For once, she did not feel let down. It almost came as a relief. If he had not suggested it, then she might have. She could tell that he felt bad about it. Despite everything that had happened, he had still not stopped being a gentleman, not entirely. She sought to reassure him.

"I'll be all right on my own here. Even in the short time that we've spent here, it has become apparent that no-one comes to much harm around here. The locals might try to sell you five bananas for five dollars and then even ask for a tip on top but they're not actually going to rob you, least of all hurt you. No, I feel quite safe here. I can look after myself. You go and have a good time! You must have already noticed how many dusky young Cuban beauties there are eyeing you up!"

At least they had managed to keep their sense of humour, almost parting on good terms. What was clearly apparent to both of them was that this was the best solution.

In a sense that holiday touring Cuba proved to be the making of her.

Not only did she stuck to her guns but travelling around alone - jumping on transport, sometimes trucks rather than buses, finding decent accommodation wherever she landed, not taking the first thing room offered, arguing the toss with the locals, bartering, even walking away if necessary - she thoroughly enjoyed the whole experience. If this was travel, if this was independent travel, then she would happily do more of it. Bring it on!

Chapter Nine

Looking back, that trip changed a lot.

In a sense it also did the opposite - just kept things the same, even more strongly. In another sense, it sort of brought her to a crossroads. She was clearly out of step. That was not exactly news, anything surprising. And going forward, there seemed to be only two possible paths. She seemed to have arrived at a fork in the road.

Down one way she could conform, adjust her thinking and her behaviour to that of the world, of modern society. That way lay advantages. She would fit in better, have an easier life. Everything would not be so much of a struggle, a fight. Why not just let her hair down and live?

Down the other path it meant saying 'Balls!' to all that and if anything becoming more herself. No compromise! No conforming! Just staying true to the little voices inside. Just staying true.

There seemed to be no third way. Even standing still seemed not an option. And typical of any fork in the road, whichever way one chose, the further one went down, the further apart the two would be, the one from the other.

No, they were two ever-diverging paths. Plus, one suspected that once engaged down the one or the other, there was little chance of a change of mind, no coming back up, no retracing steps. This seemed like a crossroads which would be life-determining.

And so it proved.

She still took up the appointment as trainee accountant at the most established firm in her university town, Durham. No, her decision would not lead her to go off and lead a hippie existence somewhere, more the opposite. She would keep believing in the traditional values of hard work and conscientiousness, of honesty and sincerity. Above all, she would do her best to stay true to herself. Her destiny was set.

Would it lead to success?

What was success? There seemed to be several kinds. There was public and private. There was western and spiritual. There was the fulfilment of emotional and physical needs and retaining one's integrity. It could be complex. More often it was delightfully simple.

Several other young men trod more or less the same path as had Benjamin.

They were from diverse backgrounds, from diverse professions. All were decent young men, who admired and respected Alexandria for her qualities. But still she was somehow, maybe only subconsciously, looking for something extra, for someone who would go that extra mile - would love her for herself and accept her exactly as she was.

Maybe she was asking for the impossible. Maybe he would have to be a saint, near perfect, combining the self-discipline of a St Paul with the patience of Job. A few millennia had elapsed since such figures had walked the earth and we would soon be entering a new one. Surely even she realised that this was no longer sustainable.

In fact, why not wise up and be aware of the times? Why not give herself until that very point in time? The turn of the next century? The turn of the next millennium?

By all means pursue her dream for the time being, for the next few years. But if she were still in the same situation when Big Ben chimed midnight on the 31st December 2000, then should she not, exactly one second later, abandon that dream, call it a day and face reality?

After all, she would no longer be a young woman any more, no longer a young innocent exactly. Would it not be time then, as a new age dawned, to throw in her hand, to admit defeat, to change sides, to get on the winning one? Did she want to be a loser all her life?

If so, then she would find herself increasingly isolated.

Was it not plain enough? - that the world did not particularly like a loser? No, it was plain that it always, increasingly, gravitated towards the winners. There the definition of success was not so complicated.

Where was the need for all the brain-racking? Why not accept life on life's terms? The world as it was? Whom did it help to stand apart? Aloof? Was she not in truth her own worst enemy? The evidence was overwhelming.

And yet the decision remained hers and hers alone.

It was not that she did not consider the evidence, look at the options. She did more than her fair share of agonising. She was not letting herself off the hook. But in the end there was always a decision to make, maybe not an easy one.

Thus far it had all been one-way traffic but that did not mean that it always had to be. She even believed fervently that there was a first time for everything. But thus far, whenever the gladiator, staring defeat in the face, appealed to the crowd, to the Emperor, rather the Empress, so far the only response had been the thumbs down. There it was again - another Benjamin bit the dust.

In the end love had not come calling, at least not her version of love, which to her was the only version.

Nothing less would do. And not even time, rushing by, could change that. No, it was not meant to be, that much was clear now. She was not part of the chosen few. She had hoped. She had dreamed. Oh, how she had dreamed! She could recount them now, describe all those pictures on her head. She had run the play through so many times as to be word-perfect.

She knew that she was capable of it - capable of loving, capable of being loved, capable of being happy, of sharing happiness. She knew all that, felt it in the very fibre of her being.

True, she had waited more than had gone looking. But at least it had been ever waiting with an open heart, ready to respond. Few open avenues had she spurned to venture down. She had shown neither timidity nor fear. She had nearly always taken the hand proffered and agreed to walk hand-in-hand down the road. The trouble was that not even at the end, only halfway down, always lay disappointment.

It was not love, real love, on offer, but something else, something disguised as love. She saw through it and once seen through, there was no going back, no going back to the naïve ignorance of before. It was another dead-end, to be dropped and put down to experience. Maybe the next one would be the real thing. Maybe.

Chapter Ten

She was mesmerised now.

If the man on the tiller had continued talking, then she would have still stopped listening to him, not a word registering. No, this was not the first time that she had seen the very same island from the very same angle. But the first time it had been different.

That first time it had just been a sort of casual, almost light-hearted exploration, almost a bit of a lark. This time it was different. This time, not only had the ownership of the island changed - to hers! - but it meant that this blob of greenery, no longer on the horizon but with every passing minute and every passing wave becoming larger and more real, was her future home.

Yes, a couple of days before, she had left home. And now she was coming home. Yes, it felt that surreal. In a sense this was the stuff of dreams. And yet it was reality, all too true. The island kept coming closer, getting bigger. Soon they were there.

They moored up.

There was a nice little jetty which meant that no-one had to get their feet wet. Everything seemed calm. Here the eastern trade winds were not so strong or rather this island was not so exposed. Nothing was rushed. That seemed to be part of the way of life in the whole region with the possible exception of the capital, which no doubt attracted Parisians, almost incapable of slowing down.

She had brought a considerable amount of provisions with her. Before setting off from Grande Terre they had loaded several boxes on to the little boat. There might also still be some crops in the ground. That was an area which she hoped to concentrate on, not exactly becoming self-sufficient but acting as a substantial supplement to supplies bought in, brought in.

There were no keys to hand over. What little paperwork that had had to be done was already completed, conducted by correspondence beforehand. In theory, the man could turn his boat right round and motor away, leaving her to own devices.

But he showed no such inclination. On the contrary, he seemed anxious to show her around again, to make sure that she settled in, knew where everything important was. Not until she was happy would he be happy, enough to feel able to leave her to it.

After unloading the boxes, they checked the freezer.

It was full to the brim. Clearly the previous owners had not exactly left in a hurry but had plainly decided that they could take nothing with them, only their clothes and most of their personal possessions. Like her back in the UK, they had even had to leave behind a substantial library. But thinking about it, it would be a happy coincidence indeed if their tastes in reading coincided with hers.

Well, at least it did not look as if she was going to starve to death, at least not in the near future. That was something at least, to set both their minds at rest. Still he was looking at her with a question mark on his face, as if he were still wondering - 'Do you really know what you are getting into, lady?' It was a good question. If he were to voice it out loud, she would most likely only be able to reply - 'Yes and no'.

In fact he was very good.

It really looked as if he had a genuine concern for her. It was one thing for a young Australian, in the prime of life and with rippling muscles, to come and try to live here, one who was eventually joined by an even younger companion from France. It was quite another thing to bring here a fairly frail-looking middle-aged Englishwoman, for all appearances past her best, certainly past her prime, who did not even look as if she had done her own weeding but had employed a gardener. His expression suggested that he was really concerned for her.

Okay, on a calm day like today, with the novelty of just arriving, with the energy that any new venture brought - of course, she would get through the coming days, maybe even the coming weeks. But then, surely, a sense of reality must set in. Maybe problems would arise, practical ones, ones which would be beyond her skills and experience.

No, this was not a difficult climate. Nevertheless, extremes of weather did happen from time to time, could be serious, with grave consequences. He and the other locals had grown up with it, were used to it, knew what to do, almost instinctively.

She, on the other hand, would literally be all at sea, at the mercy of the elements. No, it would not be as if she were shipwrecked miles from land but maybe not that much different. Then, maybe, she would have to send out an SOS call. But his alarm doubled at her next declaration.

"I've decided not to activate the communication systems."

He looked at her, even more dumbfounded. She elaborated.

"I think that it was the Frenchwoman who had it all installed - the satellite dish etc, out at the back. They subscribed to a telephone line, which gave them Internet access too. The laptop and everything are still there, I imagine in perfect working order. But I've sort of taken the decision - not to renew the subscription, in other words to live without all that means of communication."

Still he said nothing, just looking at her.

"I figured that it would be cheating somehow, almost defeating the object of what I'm trying to do here. I'd still be very much in touch with the outside world. In fact, there would be a very real temptation to continue almost with what has become a traditional western lifestyle - spending hours on the Internet, keeping in touch with the world and his wife, perhaps the first thing that you did on awakening each morning. In a way that's exactly what I'm trying to get away from, what I'm hoping to leave behind. You see, I'm seeking a greater purity, a return to naturalness. And if I had all these modern means of communication at my fingertips, then it would somehow dilute the experience, maybe even ultimately defeat it. So my decision is made."

Still he did not say anything immediately. She could almost see inside his head, see the cogs turning, the thoughts and ideas whirring around. Finally they seemed to compute.

"But what about emergencies? What if you get into a fix, have an accident? What if there is a major breakdown, say to the desalination plant, leaving you without fresh water? Have you not thought about any of that?"

She paused before replying.

"Yes, I have."

It was all that she had to say on the matter.

Nevertheless, he did not leave until he had checked everything over and thoroughly.

It was as if he now, with this new owner, felt a certain responsibility. In reality none fell on his shoulders. He had discharged his duties and admirably. Surely now he could turn and go back home, more or less wash his hands of her. If nothing else, she seemed determined, appeared to know her own mind. So why should he worry unduly? He had earned his commission. They were quits now. Over to her now, to make the best of it that she could. Still he hesitated. And indeed she did have one last request.

"Could you find it in your schedule to come back over again, say in a about month's time, or a month and a half? I've drawn up a little list here - of provisions I'll need, probably on a regular basis, things I'm likely to run out of. It's mainly booze! So just the essentials!"

She was not joking entirely.

"But if you could see your way to picking up most of these items and bringing them over, I'd be grateful. Just add on your own commission as usual and I'll settle up with you on the spot."

Still he did not say much, just nodded, as if he could not really be bothered to voice the universal reply - 'No problem!' Finally he did not seem to have much choice. There was literally nothing more to be done. Or said. All he could do now was to wish her well and leave. No, he could not even add - 'If you need anything else, just call me! If anything goes wrong, you know where I am!'

No, she was very much on her own now, beyond his help, beyond his reach. As he turned to go, he was just hoping in his mind that when he did return in a month's time, she would still be here, alive and kicking. But if he were honest with himself, he would not be able to declare that he had no doubts. On the contrary, he had plenty.

Chapter Eleven

Suddenly she felt tired.

It had been a long journey, all in all, not without its emotional side. If her first inclination was to go out and check everything out again, to explore her new possession, her second inclination was to postpone that until the morrow and just take it easy for the rest of the day. But she did allow herself another little tour of the house.

How lucky she was in a sense! Probably twenty years ago this was just a shack, with no running water, with no electricity, with no domestic appliances, with nothing resembling modern creature comforts. Now look at it!

It must have been the influence of the Frenchwoman, she thought, looking around. Not only was there nothing lacking, there had been so much attention to detail. In the end, the couple had wanted for nothing, had a lifestyle more western than third world.

For him, the Australian, in particular, it must have felt like coming full circle. Twenty-odd years before, he had turned his back on this lifestyle, had deliberately gone off somewhere remote to rediscover the primitive life. And he had found it, without doubt, living off Nature, living by his wits.

No doubt it was the fulfilment of some sort of dream and no doubt he found the sense of peace and fulfilment which he was seeking. No doubt that feeling of fulfilment was further enhanced when one of few surprise visitors decided to stay on. They found love together. His cup must have run over.

And who could blame them if in time they wanted to live less like Spartans, less like primitives in the jungle? If she brought a bit of a stack of money with her, then why not spend it? - To make life a little bit easier, more comfortable and interesting? Maybe in the end the process had led them to want to rejoin the human race.

There was no shame in that. In a sense he had done his thing, completed his project. What was certain was that he would have learned one heck of a lot, maybe enough now to equip him to live in the outside world. He could, they both could, go back and face it now as self-sufficient, picking and choosing, do it on their terms. Life went in cycles sometimes. That was theirs.

As everywhere, in the kitchen she found every facility, even the wine rack well stocked.

It was not all French but quite an eclectic mix, including some local wines, presumably the better ones. But just for now Alexandria thought that she would stay traditional, stay within the familiar. She chose a bottle of red, origin from the Corbières, a region she knew reasonably well and whose plentiful wine output she had tasted before.

Predictably perhaps, some of the furniture was outside. A three-piece suite - a three-seater canapé plus two matching armchairs - was placed in a semicircle around a long slim low coffee table. In another shaded corner of the garden was a higher table, more for dining, surrounded by four upright chairs, only two of which had seen much use.

She settled back into one of the armchairs in the garden, facing south, one she remembered sitting in on her first visit, the 'recky' some months before. From there she could see the bay, the blue water stretching to the far horizon. It looked so beautiful and peaceful.

She took a sip of wine. Nectar! How come she had taken so long to discover it? When she thought back to all those boring parties which she had had to attend, no wonder all the others had seemed to thoroughly enjoy themselves, knocking back the stuff as if there were no tomorrow, leaving her stone cold sober and bored, she always the first to leave at the flimsiest of excuses.

Maybe, just maybe, if by some miracle she had her life to live over again, she would do it just a little differently, perhaps make just a slightly bigger effort to have what people called fun. But she would not live it entirely differently. In fact, even thinking about it now, wineglass in hand, before a magnificent view of the ocean, she would not change the essentials.

In particular, she did not regret not having married. Or rather not having cohabited. Her ideals, though not realised, still remained intact. Never had she come even close to abandoning them, to modifying them. Was that not after all why she found herself here now? No, even as a mature woman, certainly more than halfway through her earthly existence, still she was not going to give in, throw in the towel, hand over her soul.

Nor was she going to judge anyone else.

Each person decided their own life, how they lived it, according to what code. She had no quarrel with that. She liked to see people enjoying themselves and if they could find happiness on that other path, then good luck to them!

But she could not, never would. So she had been obliged to stay true to herself, right to the end. Now this was the end, it seemed. Maybe she would now live out the rest of her days here in peace and tranquillity, with no further conflicts to trouble her, no tricky decisions, in particular without censure from others outside.

No, she could now look around and say to herself - 'I am the Queen of all that I survey!' She was. And if it felt just slightly bitter-sweet, then she still found a way of passing a small smile across her wine-stained lips. She had a confession to make.

It was only a detail but it was something which she had insisted on. To the bureaucrats receiving the request, it must have caused more amusement than concern. It must have caused them to scratch their heads in puzzlement and indeed wonder what strange minds there were abroad in the world, particularly in the west. It probably convinced them that they were better off where they were - stuck on an island in the middle of the Pacific Ocean, well away from all perversity.

The island was called 'Motu Moemoea', translated officially as 'Îlot des Rêves', 'Islet of Dreams'. But the condition of purchase which Alexandria laid down, one on which she insisted, even called 'not negotiable', was that the name be changed, if only slightly. On the land transfer deed, she was now designated as the owner of 'Îlot des Rêves Brisés'.

Suddenly she stood up from the armchair in the corner of the garden, overlooking the bay and the blue ocean, more leapt to her feet. Her back was straight, her chest thrust out, the half-empty wine glass still in her right hand. She raised it to the sky, downed the rest of the contents in one and spake out loud.

"Here's to the future! On the Islet of Broken Dreams!"

Chapter Twelve

Her first supper was a simple affair.

She prepared an omelette accompanied by a mixed salad, laced with her own special vinaigrette sauce. Her many travels through France had not been wasted. One of many kind hostesses had been keen to show her how - exactly which ingredients to use and then in what precise proportions. The best vinaigrette ever made in France, the hostess had claimed. Alexandria was not inclined to disbelieve her.

All in all, she counted her first evening in her new home a pleasant one. She slept surprisingly well. Maybe the wine helped. Okay, it was over a long period, accompanying her evening meal and then finally as a nightcap, but she managed to polish off the whole bottle.

She awoke early.

Maybe this would become the pattern. Generally speaking it was only in sophisticated societies, the drift to late nights and late mornings. The rustic way of life had always been the opposite - early to bed and early to rise.

Okay, originally it might have been in order to maximise the use of natural daylight and to save on the expense of artificial light. Here in her situation, with solar-energy-generated electricity on permanent tap and inexhaustible, that was clearly not going to be an issue. But it seemed natural, on her first morning, to rise early, not exactly with the sun but before it was high in the sky.

After a light breakfast and a couple of pots of tea it was finally time to venture outside.

It was time for her to familiarise herself with her new home surroundings. Looking around, it was like having a massive garden. In whichever direction she walked, she was on home territory. It felt weird at first.

Part of it was garden. And part of the garden was orchard, or allotment, with all sorts growing. There were banana trees, mangoes, yams, sweet potato. Most of the stuff she admitted that she did not recognise but it certainly looked good enough to eat.

She imagined that the freezer would be mainly stocked with meat because there was certainly an abundance of vegetables growing outside. Thinking about it, she doubted even if there would be any frozen fish in it.

Knowing the previous owners, or rather, not knowing them personally but piecing together how they were, how they lived, there was bound to be fishing tackle stashed away somewhere in one of the outbuildings. What more pleasant way to spend an afternoon than sitting on the jetty and casting a line? Or even taking the rowing boat out on the calm waters and trying her luck further out?

She continued her exploration.

Wherever she looked, there was always something, it seemed, to bring a smile to her face. This was not the bleak austerity of a North Yorkshire hill farm in winter but just about the opposite, something closer to a tropical paradise. Everything seemed gentle, in its place, part of a coherent whole.

Yet she found so many apparent incongruities. Some of the outbuildings were still somewhat ramshackle. She noticed that they were secured against high wind but they still kept their rustic charm. Other buildings, no doubt more recent, were largely to western standards, built on a solid base, if looking rather indigenous, say with a thick grass roof. And then, quite abruptly, the cultivated garden suddenly gave way to what she could only describe as jungle. At least there were paths. She decided to follow one.

Soon she was really in the thick of it.

The vegetation was truly dense. Someone once had clearly had to cut their way through, literally with a machete. Even so, some of the leaves on either side were really sharp. Clearly jungles knew how to defend themselves. Even on a path she would have to exercise considerable care.

On she walked, losing track of both time and distance. How big was the island? She could scarcely remember. Was it 2.8 km²? Or 5.6 km²? It was one or the other. Just now, trekking on through the dense growth, she was inclined to think that it was the larger of the two.

Theoretically, sooner or later and probably sooner, she would come to the end of it, come to the end of the island, to another beach, at least to water. That was the main feature about islands - that they were bordered on all sides by water - sea or ocean - were finite in that sense.

She understood how islands unnerved some people, because in a sense they were ringed, sort of fenced off, with no natural means to continue, to escape. She felt the opposite, the security of a specific limited area. She wanted to be fenced in in some strange way. She had no desire to continue on or escape.

In a way she had already done her escaping - away from her own land, her old life. This precisely was what she was escaping to. It made all the difference in the world. She was not hemmed in. On the contrary, she was free. And that was how it felt.

Unexpectedly, she came upon a small clearing.

It looked half natural, half man-made, as if there had originally been a small one, now enlarged. To her even greater surprise, she looked across and up and found herself staring at a treehouse.

It looked so cute, quite small, just perched up there, resting on the first substantial branches. A little rustic-made ladder, held together by tree fibres, invited access. Needless to say, she could not resist the temptation and was soon gingerly climbing up.

Fairly predictably, it just consisted of one room. It was light and airy, with no glass in the windows on each side. Looking up, she wondered if the roof would be fully waterproof. But then, on second thoughts, where was the need, out here, most of the time?

It was sparsely furnished. There was a small table and two upright chairs, clearly all home-made but strong, serviceable. In the other corner sat an easy chair, offering more comfort. And then - the crowning glory - all along one side lay a low bed, wooden, of course, on the top of which sat a thin-looking mattress, halfway between a single and a double.

The whole scene looked so sweet, so idyllic. It must be so nice to spend the night out here, on the north side of the island, completely isolated but in this really cosy treehouse. Maybe she would one day, just for the change, just for the experience. It would be like being a kid again, camping in the woods, getting close to Nature, having only other creatures for companions, hopefully no nasty little ones.

She rejoined the path. It was back into dense undergrowth again. The trouble was that she could not see far ahead. There was no way of knowing what was round the next corner, even how far it would be to the water's edge. But that had to come up, sooner or later.

Eventually it did.

One minute she was fighting her way through a mass of jungle plants, the next an opening in the trees appeared and through it she could see blue beyond. Not only that, as she emerged through the opening, she found herself standing on a narrow strip of sand whiter than her own feet. It was truly beautiful. Now that she was out there, by the water's edge, even that seemed more green than blue now. Was this truly paradise? It was not far short.

As she turned to walk along the beach, it broadened out. The shape of the shore resembled another bay. She could not resist the temptation to walk along it. She would even walk in the water. How good that felt! The water was warm. It was as if it were friendly. In fact, thinking about it now, even this early on, did that not describe the whole island? Friendly? She even said it out loud -

"I think that we are going to be good friends, very good friends!"

Chapter Thirteen

Halfway round the bay, looking inland towards the forest, she spotted something else unusual, nay extraordinary.

Just in the shade of the last line of trees there stood a small round grass-topped beach hut. They really had been busy bees, the previous owners. Or did this too date back to the man's solo era, he perhaps hoping back then, if not eventually to find someone to share the island with, a partner, at least hoping to have a few visitors from time to time. And what better idea than to have little living spaces dotted about - a charming little treehouse there, a neat little beach hut here, so inviting.

Once again she could not resist the temptation. She pushed the door open. The interior was not dissimilar from the one which she had just seen. Along one side was a long bench with cushions on it. At a pinch, it could double up as a bed of sorts.

There was even a little wooden cupboard with a few kitchen utensils inside - mugs, bowls, plates and cutlery, all unusually made out of wood. Alexandria was thinking that they must be examples of local craftsmanship. They looked beautiful. She would not dare use them but would prefer to keep them for decoration. Maybe when she came back to the beach hut another day she would bring with her more conventionally made crockery and cutlery.

That seemed enough for a first morning's exploration.

Now she would slowly wend her way back to the main house. She smiled. Would she find her way back all right? Or would she get lost in the jungle? It was a thought. Even on a small island, particularly one as overgrown as this, preventing one from having views of the rest, it might easily be possible to get lost. Going back she would simply try to stick rigidly to the path and then just hope for the best.

Maybe it just appeared to take a bit longer, getting back. And it was with some relief that, turning a bend, she saw a little more light ahead, saw ground which opened up, looked more like garden than forest.

It felt time for lunch.

She would leave the wine in its rack today, at least until later. Once again she prepared something simple. It looked as if she was going to get to like, or at least get used to, mixed salad with a good French vinaigrette sauce. She decided to eat it outside under the shade of the coolibah tree. As everywhere she had a view of the ocean, so blue. Gazing at it, she was unable to stop her mind from wandering.

'So far, so good! I know that it's early days, less than twenty-four hours that I have spent in my new home, in my new country, but I can't honestly say that I'm in anyway disappointed. That is always the fear. The question is always - was that first visit a bit like a fantasy, your head turned, a bit carried away, intoxicated by the sea air? Would the reality, second time around, be different? Would then the sheer practicalities or impracticalities impinge and spoil that first idyllic picture, not so much turn the project sour but bring reservations, serious ones? But I can honestly say that I don't feel like that. If anything the place is even more beautiful than I thought the first time around. It is a kind of paradise. There's no getting away from it. It's like a Garden of Eden. Like the original Garden of Eden there is everything one could possibly need here. Like it too, it is almost like a place of innocence, not exactly virgin but retaining much of the original purity. Maybe I've just got to hope that there are no ripe apples to pick, that there is no sinister tree lurking somewhere, the one of knowledge of good and evil.'

She allowed a wry smile to pass across her lips. Original sin? Guilt? No, she had her belief system, a sincerely held one, but there was no room in it for all that stuff.

'I know that the world can be a hard and sometimes even cruel place. But I still believe that there are pockets of goodness and innocence somewhere. In fact, I hope that I have found one here.'

Nor did she dodge the big question.

'Yes, it would be even better, even more fulfilling, to be sharing all this beauty, to be sharing it with a dear one. All my life I've believed in sharing, probably even believed that it was the number one prize in life, even if, looking back, I don't seem to have done much of it. Of course, I would like to have shared my life with someone. That was always the dream. But it didn't come true. The reality now is that I have no-one to share this with. So I must learn to appreciate it without sharing it. I do already. I have come home. And that's how it feels.'

She got into a routine in no time at all.

She did not have much fixed mealtimes, just ate when she felt hungry, drank when she felt thirsty. Most evenings she allowed herself a couple of glasses of wine. One bottle did her for two nights. It did enhance the evening meal, indeed enhance the evening.

One pleasure which she soon discovered was taking an outside shower.

It was not even necessary to heat the water. No walls, not even chest-high, had been built around the shower to hide anyone's modesty. It seemed so liberating somehow to be out there in the open air, in the buff, as naked as a child, wallowing in the pleasure of the flowing water, getting clean at the same time. Yes, if there was a lost innocence, surely she was winning it back now.

She had been right about the fishing.

In one of the huts she found a variety of fishing tackle. In the library she even found a book on it. Never having done any fishing before in her life, she needed all the instruction that she could get. In particular, she knew instinctively that good baiting would be important, would make the difference between success and failure.

The idea did not appeal at first but eventually she decided to face it and get her hands dirty. She managed to dig up some worms and even managed to bait her hooks with them. But it proved worth it. In the course of her first afternoon, sitting quietly on the jetty with a couple of lines dangling in the water, she eventually got a bite. She grabbed the rod and just about succeeded in landing a real fish, her first.

She figured that it was a small emperor fish. Another book found on the shelves gave instructions on how to gut it, fillet it and cook it. That would be this evening's task. Overall, she was learning fast.

Everything was new, different.

She was doing so many things which she had never done before, never even thought about. They were only simple pleasures, nothing to write home about. Others would laugh at the tingle of excitement which she was often feeling.

Sure, it was the novelty of it all. But that surely would wear off in no time at all, probably before the man on the tiller was back again. She would soon get fed up of gutting fish and washing vegetables. It would soon become a drag, gathering in heavy baskets of fruit, trimming the grass, burying the rubbish.

But somehow it did not. Each day she could honestly say to herself that she relished every task before her. No, it was not play. Yes, it was work, some of it hard work. Sometimes, afterwards she was dog-tired and had to rest for the remainder of the day. But she could honestly say that she did everything with a light heart, with the opposite of a heavy one.

Chapter Fourteen

It was difficult to keep track of the days.

There was, literally, nothing to remind her, nothing to check on. It almost seemed ridiculous. Back in the world where she had just come from, one could almost not avoid knowing the day, the date, even the time. They were, literally, the elements which governed lives.

Now, suddenly, all that was absent. One day merged into another. There were not really weekends. If she wanted, she could let Christmas Day come and go without even being aware of it. What about the years? Would she continue to keep track of those? Would she even remember her own birthday? It was strange, almost funny.

She decided to make a calendar.

It was another thing to do, a fun thing but useful. Like many of the home-made things about the place, she would try to make it out of wood. She would carve a suitable amount of letters and numbers and somehow put them on a board, showing the day of the week, the initial letter or two, the month, the initial letter or two, the date and finally the year.

Although back home she had always, unlike most, when writing, included the initial '20' in the year, here she decided to let herself off such obligation. She had lived through one change of century. It was very unlikely that she would live through another.

She took a surprising amount of trouble.

In a sense, there was no need. After all, most likely no-one other than she was ever likely to clap eyes on it, to check it, to keep it up-to-date. But something drove her somehow to keep working on those numbers and letters, getting them just right, till they were even things of beauty. She even gave them a final polish in palm oil.

When she finally decided that it was finished, she accorded it prime position in the lounge, such that it was unmissable. That way, she hoped, she would not omit to update it daily. She also felt a sneaking dram of pride about it. Why should she not give it pride of place? Her first real creation? In the end she could not stop looking at it. In the end she did stop.

Still, even with the new calendar, even if she did manage to keep it bang up-to-date, still she did not know exactly when the man would return in his little boat.

After all, she had only asked him to return 'in about a month's time'. Add on to that the more laissez-faire attitude towards things like time generally in this part of the world and there was no way of knowing exactly what interpretation he would put on it, what priority he would give it. Perhaps even, to him it meant nothing more than 'in a month or two'.

If so, it was not of much consequence. She was not running low on anything, on anything vital. Rather the contrary - with each passing day she seemed to be aware of even more bounty around. If anything she was developing a preference for things home-grown. At this rate, even, there might be the possibility of becoming virtually self-sufficient one day.

On the other hand, there would always be certain foodstuffs, or drinks, which she could never make herself. And maybe she would not want to lose that last final contact, seeing the face of the man on the tiller every month or two. She had not gone to the moon after all, not quite.

Thinking about it, maybe she could one day turn her hand to making wine, or even beer. By all accounts it was not that difficult. Okay, grapes were not growing in abundancc but there were plenty of other fruits around. In theory you could make wine out of anything. Back home she knew that people brewed their own home beer.

She might not be able to get hold of exactly the right materials but it might be worth a bash. Who knew with time? But just for now she seemed to be living in the land of plenty. In fact, it seemed that, wherever she looked, around every corner there was something new which she had not seen before.

In the hut where she had found the fishing tackle there was another huge refrigerator. Stood there, she just assumed that it had become surplus to requirements. Maybe it did not work any more but had simply been discarded, removed from the house and just dumped somewhere where there was a bit of space. So far she had not even been bothered going to the trouble of opening it.

But when one day she did, not only did she find it to be in perfect working order, connected to the power supply and set to a good low temperature, in addition it was full. And what of? - Nothing but tins and tins of the finest lager beer!

It seemed that the previous owner, our Australian friend, having turned his back on his homeland and its way of life, still held on to one of its traditions and quite tightly. No wonder he had needed a bigger boat! - not only to bring over these bigger appliances in the first place but then to transport the wherewithal to fill them!

It was another drink which she had never really given a chance to.

She had sometimes felt tempted, particularly on a hot summer's day, spending time with friends, not inside the pub but outside in the beer garden. She had sometimes looked longingly at the cool glasses of her friends and wondered how refreshing that would be, also how convivial. Yet for some reason she had always resisted the temptation. Maybe she was regretting that now.

Today the climatic conditions were not dissimilar. It was warm, the sun beating down. If she were going to keep the wine for the evenings, then maybe she could allow herself a long cool lager at lunchtime. She was feeling tempted. This time, unlike before, she gave in to temptation. She went and sat down in a chair on the lawn next to the low table.

Yes, it tasted just as good as she anticipated. It was cool. It was long. It was clean. It was refreshing. In addition, it was just a little so ever intoxicating. It felt so nice, just like the wine. She felt so relaxed, at peace with everything.

The world of work was behind her now. That seemed to make the difference. No longer was she at the beck and call of anyone, always obliged to turn up every morning, spruce, alert. Here, now, there were no expectations on her, none. There were no work obligations any longer.

There were no expectations - from others. Above all, there was no-one watching now, whether she was taking a brazen shower outside in the nuddy or, as now, opening a tinnie of cold lager and letting the contents slowly run down her throat. Soon the can was drained.

If she was free now, then why not live it? - the free life? Surely she had earned it. She had done her stint, done the correct thing, all the correct things. But now, surely, it was time to change.

No, she was not going to go wild, start to live a dissolute life. She never had liked parties and she was not going to start now. No, that was the whole point of coming here, of going off alone. But surely now she could let her hair down a little, not watching herself as much. If no-one else was watching, then why should she? There had to be small pleasures in life.

In fact, since her arrival she was finding many. So why not add one or two more? There was no-one imposing any limit, only herself. Even she now must see that little purpose would be served by continuing to be Little Miss Strict. Those days were gone now too. If she was going to change lifestyle, then she might just as well do it completely.

She could even walk around in the nude if she chose.

In fact, why not do that very thing and get a lovely all-over tan without the need for the ugly lines, the white bits spoiling the effect? No-one was to know. Even if she were to do that very thing on the very day that the man on the tiller arrived, she would get plenty of warning in advance, hearing in the silence the chug-chug of his engine from far out, time enough to nip inside and put something on, appear decent.

Even that was a bit of a misnomer. Was she not decent already? Even in the nude? Letting the air to her body? To the whole of it? She lived in the sun now, so was it not right for her body to be exposed to it? To enjoy it? Was it not almost incumbent upon her now to enjoy everything that she could?

She had served her time and now she had been let out, freed. Did she not owe it to herself now to enjoy that freedom? One hundred percent? After living fifty years one way, it was never going to be easy to flip over and live another. But if, as she claimed, she truly did have an open mind, then even that should be possible.

"Fuck it!"

She had said it once before, in fact not so very long ago, only a matter of days. This time anyone in the close vicinity would have heard it. She went back inside the hut and emerged a few seconds later, her hands no longer empty. She took off all her clothes and threw them on the grass. She sat down again in the corner of the lawn next to the small table. She could see the blue water ahead. She reached out and drew a second ring-pull.

Chapter Fifteen

Weeks passed, even months.

If it were not for the calendar, which she meticulously updated each day, she would have no idea how many, absolutely no idea of time passing, how much.

It was not as if there were much seasonal variation. True, there were slight variations of temperature between the seasons but not so much. Most rain fell in the summer months, the warmest. It was towards the end, almost into autumn, round about March time, that the winds sometimes got up more than usual, when even a full-blown cyclone could hit, sometimes with devastating results.

The previous owners had done a good job of making the whole place as cyclone-proof as possible. Sometimes the best solution was to let things bend with the wind. Those that could not were better firmly fixed down. She resolved at the beginning of the New Year to make a full inspection and take whatever measures necessary accordingly.

Meanwhile she was enjoying the peace and quiet.

There was something else which, perhaps unexpectedly, she was enjoying - the absence of news. Even 'back home', while still working, still not so very long ago, how many times had she resolved to watch less TV, in particular to watch less of the news, even to cut it out entirely?

There was rarely anything uplifting to be seen or heard on it. Increasingly it was largely about political argument, ideological discussion, rarely leading to any agreement, more towards ever increasing polarisation.

In a word, everyone seemed to be just squabbling. It was depressing. She would be doing herself a favour by switching to another channel, by watching another type of programme. Maybe the biggest favour that she could do herself would be by pressing the 'off' button. And then not touching it again.

Certainly, now, she found that she did not miss it. Now she had no way of knowing - what was going on in the outside world. Was there war? Revolution? Certainly, she could not imagine that a new era of co-operation had dawned. No, it appeared that man, and woman, preferred to fight than to peacefully coexist.

But she had left all that behind now. For her, in a sense, mankind could, if it wished, go ahead and destroy itself. It would be sad indeed. It was sad already, what was happening, the way it was happening. Put it like this - there was much more happiness available to mankind than was actually being enjoyed.

But that was not her doing. On the contrary, she could honestly say that she had done her best, at all times and in all places, to bring other people pleasure more than pain. She had always tried to be considerate, conscious of other people's feelings. In particular, she had avoided all argument.

She had always hated hearing people rowing. Of course, the worst nearly always occurred within families, even between couples, so-called loving ones. Whenever she heard a couple rowing, whether she knew them or not, it always cut her to the quick.

She would remain upset for the rest of the day. The rowing, the screaming, would stay in her mind, repeating itself. It was like darts, pricking at her heart. She hated it. She resolved that she would never do it. She never had.

But now she was away from all that. Couples could tear themselves apart if they wanted. The whole world could tear itself apart if it wanted. She wanted no part of it, not any more. She had voted with her feet, turned her back on it. So far she was not regretting it.

There was one luxury which she permitted herself.

On her very first visit she had noticed the laptop, even if she had already decided against it, in terms of a means of communication with the outside world. But what had caught her eye was a modest set of loudspeakers, to which it was connected, all three looking remarkably modern.

Largely gone were the days of the old large loudspeaker. New technologies had reduced the size, as they had in other fields like computers and smart phones. She had not tried them out but she suspected that the set-up could produce quite a rich sound.

After that it was not difficult - more the easiest thing in the world - before departure from home, to load up a small number of high capacity memory sticks. She could have even brought a stack of films to watch. But she chose only to bring music.

It was an eclectic mix. It was not that she was indiscriminate, liked everything. But in a curious sort of way she had always found herself equally excited by rock music as classical. It was the same ears that heard, the same heart that vibrated, the same excitement that she felt. So during her final months back in the old country, she had meticulously copied to the drives all her favourite music.

There was perhaps one other luxury.

On her travels she had long since dispensed with taking books with her for reading material, physical books, even lightweight paperbacks. Instead she carried a reading tablet. It worked pretty well. In fact, it was the perfect traveller's friend. Once again, during her final months, she decided to load up the tablet, just about to its full capacity.

She made a decision - that she would simply load up all the free classics. It was not that she was unwilling to spend any money, more that it would be so difficult, so time-consuming, to go through the millions of titles of more contemporary novels. This way she kept it super-simple. It was all done and dusted in remarkably short time.

Chapter Sixteen

She chose to do her main tasks in the mornings.

That was when she felt the freshest, when she felt she had the most energy, so it was the best time for doing any hard labour. If she had any digging to do, any heavy carrying, then she would make sure that it was completed by the end of the morning, otherwise she would postpone it till the morrow.

Yes, she liked work and always had. But she always knew, even before she tried it, that part-time work would be a ton better than full-time. So it proved. Come midday, roughly, she would finish her present task, pack up for the day, put the tools away and wander slowly back to the house. Lunch was soon prepared. It was time for a light leisurely midday meal. She knew the moves. It was almost like some kind of ritual.

She would open the laptop and select a piece of music, a composer or a collection, if it were pop/rock. She might choose Vaughan Williams or Prokofiev, Queen or one of the later groups, or even one of the earlier groups, or one of the more recent female soloists. She would open her reading tablet and select a novel or, more often, find the place where she had left off reading her current one. She would go to the outhouse where stood the big upright fridge and take out a tinnie of lager.

Then she would find her spot - nearly always the same - seated on an easy chair next to the low table, in the shade of the coolibah tree. She was set up - not just for lunchtime but for the best part of the afternoon. No, it was not paradise. But it was not a bad imitation.

The visits from the man on the tiller did begin to stretch out.

The norm became once every two months. On one occasion he left it for a full three.

He knew by now that she was all right, that she could fend for herself. To put it one way - she was not going to run out of anything vital. She had a plentiful supply of fresh water. The freezer was always kept well stocked. She was getting better and better at growing vegetables and gathering fruits. She was becoming a dab hand at catching small fish. Thus far she did not look like running out of drink.

She had been joking that first time but the reality was that, when he did visit now, probably 50% of his cargo was accounted for by wine and lager. They still joked about it. She joked that she was well on the way to becoming a closet alchy. He always reassured her.

"You've got nothing on these Parisians who come over. Many drink like fish. Or as they themselves say sometimes - 'Ils boivent comme un trou' - 'Drink like a hole'. It's not just them. It's the majority of the visitors, from everywhere. We get a lot from Australia and New Zealand. They can knock it back too, I can tell you. In fact, the man who lived here, your predecessor, I saw his consumption rise over the years. That was why he had the large upright fridge brought over. He preferred lager. She, the Frenchwoman, preferred wine. They were having deliveries made more often than once every two or three months, I can tell you."

She smiled. She was not worried really. On the contrary, she was rather pleased that she had discovered this little pleasure in life. The timing seemed perfect. At the age of fifty she had stopped working, had effectively got out of the rat race. Now she led a new pace of life, more leisurely. It was a lifestyle into which a bit of moderate drinking fitted perfectly. But was hers moderate? Just for now she would take his reassurance that it was. She smiled again.

She looked at the calendar one day.

Soon would loom up an important day. In the event she had celebrated Christmas, then New Year, then her birthday. They had been modest celebrations by anyone's standards.

There was just one bottle of spirits which had been left behind by the previous owners - a bottle of whisky, a single malt, twelve years old, unopened. In the run-up to her first Christmas on Motu Moemoea she thought about it. Should she? Just one? Just to celebrate Christmas? So on the day she broke the seal, unscrewed the cap and poured herself a small one.

"Merry Christmas, Alexandria!"

It tasted beautiful, went down a treat, so smooth. She did the same on New Year's Eve, at midnight.

"Happy New Year, Alexandria!"

It tasted equally good. Not long after that she was taking her third small glass, making another toast.

"Happy Birthday, Alexandria!"

Now, as summer slipped towards autumn, she would have cause for another celebration, perhaps the most important of all. No, it would not be for April Fools' Day. But not long after - the first anniversary of her arrival on the Islet of Broken Dreams. She even made herself a secret promise - two small glasses for this celebration!

Really? A whole year?

She could barely believe it. A whole year!

In some ways it had passed quickly, all too quickly. In another sense it had passed so slowly. Yes, she was in the habit of saying that one day ran into another, with not a lot of difference between them. On the other hand, it was as if she could almost count out those 365 days, describe each one.

People said that, as you got older, time speeded up. For her it seemed the opposite. If anything, time was slowing down. She was relishing it, savouring it, just as much she was relishing and savouring these two lovely small glasses of malt whisky.

"Happy First Anniversary, Alexandria!"

Chapter Seventeen

The first visitors came as something of a shock.

Naturally, there was no way of giving Alexandria any prior warning, of asking her permission first. The boat arrived one day, fairly well on schedule, laden with the usual provisions. The difference was that the man on the tiller was not alone.

The trouble was that now, almost faced with a fait accompli, she did not really have much time to make a proper decision. She could not very well interview the couple. The man on the tiller, who was presumably collecting a nice commission out of the whole visit, was anxious to explain.

"It won't be for a month. I'll come back before then. These people have telephone coverage and can contact me at any point. They might only want to stay for a week, two at the most. Plus, we've brought over plenty of provisions, have even tried to make most of it lightweight, therefore portable. With any luck, all they'll need is access to a daily supply of drinking water. That shouldn't be too bad, should it?"

All she could do was lay down some hastily thought up rules. The first thing that came to mind was - the last thing that she wanted was their staying too close. There was loads of living space in the main house and in the wooden huts all dotted around the garden, all affording more than adequate accommodation for independent travellers. But just in this short space of time, she had sort of become jealous, protective of her own privacy. The thought ran through my mind - 'I might now have to choose my times for having showers outside in the nuddy.'

"A condition would have to be that you stuck mainly to the north of the island. There's a treehouse and a beach hut, both offering perfectly adequate sleeping accommodation. You could call around here, say, once a day, say around noon, to pick up a container of fresh water. But apart from that, I wouldn't want you to be too invasive."

It was agreed.

These coins were always double-sided. She had even thought of it before - that it might even be quite nice to have visitors from time to time. The trouble with that was that you could not pick and choose. You just had to take pot luck. Your guests might turn out to be super. On the other hand, they might turn out to be a pain in the proverbial.

The trouble was that there was no code any more. The world had grown so selfish. Maybe now independent travellers were even the worst breed of all. They seemed to believe that they had to really toughen up, which inevitably went a step further into not giving a damn about anyone else. Alexandria had seen it so many times on her own travels. She was not impressed.

All she could do was try it. If the first visit went well, then maybe she would accept a second. If that went well, then maybe she would accept a third. And so on. In a sense she must guard against the other scenario - the visit which did not go so well, the one which did create problems, the bad outweighing the good. There she might have to put that one down to experience, in other words not necessarily let it put her off completely, to the point of discontinuing all visits.

She knew better than anyone - that this crazy old world, particularly this crazy new world, was full of such a mixed bag that it had become almost impossible to navigate through. Why else would she be living now on a little island in the middle of the Pacific Ocean?

Alexandria had to admit that this first visit was working out pretty well.

She found them a very sympathetic couple, French, originally from the Loire Valley. They respected her space totally. Bang on the stroke of noon every day they would appear to collect a container of fresh water, which they could carry away on their backs. But they never stayed long.

Inevitably, without wishing to importune her, they engaged in a little conversation. Inevitably, they were so curious, as to the how and the why, of her coming to live in such a remote spot. They were really interested. And Alexandria found herself taking pleasure in explaining to them. Unusually, they seemed to understand.

When on the fifth day they called for the water, she invited them to stay a while, to share a drink. They did so gladly. It became a habit and the conversation spread to other matters, everything. It came out that they too did not feel a hundred percent comfortable, living in western Europe.

"France in particular," began Delphine, "seems to have become a hotbed for strife, all kinds of it - domestic, industrial, political. If anything, it's getting worse. Put it like this - it would come as a surprise to no-one if one day soon, say within the next decade, the French people elected a government which we would describe as extreme. It will happen, I'm sure, I mean within our lifetime. Goodness knows what sort of world it will lead to. Will we recognise France any more? - as that land of fairness, tolerance and freedom? - 'Liberté, Égalité, Fraternité'?"

Alexandria was equally interested in their story. Christophe went on.

"We've found ourselves moving further and further up the Loire Valley. We started in Nantes but now we are living in a little-known village in the hills, where the river is quite narrow. We make, rather scratch, a living by making and selling things, 'artisanerie'. As you can imagine, the winter half of the year is pretty lean. We depend on tourists, both French and foreign. But it's difficult to make ends meet. We can only make this voyage because last year Delphine's father died and unexpectedly left us a small fortune. We had no idea beforehand. He lived so frugally and we didn't think that he had two ha'pennies, or rather two centimes, to rub together. But it turned out that he was loaded. He just saved everything, put it in the bank. Now we, not he, are the beneficiaries."

Delphine took it up again.

"So we are determined to see a bit of the world, while we can. In our circumstances, it makes sense to take time off during the winter, which explains our presence here now."

"But we soon got fed up of the capital here, Nouméa." Christophe almost interrupted. "It's too geared up for tourism for our tastes, almost reminding us of France," he added with a smile. "That's why we decided to see if we could find somewhere quieter, like an outlying island."

"And we are so glad that we have!" It was Delphine's turn to interrupt. "Already these past few days have absolutely made our holiday, already made it memorable. You live in a beautiful place. Don't ever leave it!"

"In fact," concluded Christophe, "it has set our minds thinking. Maybe, when we come to retire, maybe we could do something similar. It is certainly food for thought. I imagine that on our return flight back home we'll be talking about nothing else."

Chapter Eighteen

It was such a pleasant interlude.

Alexandria probably had not realised exactly how much she had missed good company. In truth, she had spent over a year and a half without any. Now she noticed how much she did miss it, still hankered after it. On the other hand, she had made her choice, had no reason to regret it and intended to stick with it.

On the day before the couple's departure, she decided to pre-empt them.

She walked across the island in the mid-morning. She even decided to take with her a container of fresh water, to save them the trouble. But it would also mean that they would not stay for a pre-lunch drink and a chat. She had something else in mind.

"Would you like to share dinner tonight?"

At first they looked a little startled. Clearly they had not been expecting the invitation. But they were not slow to accept.

"With pleasure," they both replied, almost in unison.

"Come over about seven. It will be nothing grand, probably most of it cold. But we can make it a leisurely meal, à la Française. See you later!"

Come the evening they were as prompt as usual.

They even brought a bottle of wine with them, local produce but certain, in this environment, to taste every bit as good as anything from the cellars of the best Vignobles of France. They spent the most pleasant of evenings together.

"Well, Mademoiselle Alexandria," concluded Delphine, "we've both decided that you're incredibly brave!"

She did not feel it. She never had. She had just tried to stick to her convictions, plus, perhaps unusually, translate them into action. At the same time, it was an epithet, a word, which always seemed to be a bit double-edged. Often the implication was something more like - 'You've really stuck your neck out! Much more than most would dare, including us!' Sometimes the insinuation was that the person had been too brave, too brave for their own good.

"It's true that it will be a little easier for you and Christophe, being a couple, I mean, together. That way big steps don't seem quite so daunting. Plus, if things do start to go a bit wrong, you've still got each other. It's always more fruitful to dialogue with another person than with oneself. If the worse comes to the worst, the one can always blame the other - 'Whose idea was this in the first place?' " She was smiling. "That is a luxury denied me, of course. I've only got myself to blame."

"Or to congratulate!" Christophe almost corrected her. "I mean - in this case you've got to take all the credit. I mean - you've really come up trumps, hit the jackpot. Your boldness, your singleness of purpose, have been rewarded, one hundred percent. I just hope, come the time, that Delphine and I find the same determination, the same resolve."

"I'm sure you will. I think I know you well enough to see that you feel things quite keenly too, are very motivated. Plus, you can encourage each other, lift each other's spirits, if necessary."

"That's all the more reason," continued Delphine, "why your project, your seeing it through, should be all the more lauded. You've really followed your star. You really are a star!"

Needless to say, Alexandria was left with a permanent invitation to visit a little-known village in the upper Loire Valley.

All parties knew that she was extremely unlikely to take it up but it was a welcome gesture nevertheless. When the boat arrived, there was not much chance to speak to the man on the tiller but it was apparent to all concerned that the visit had gone well. No doubt during the boat ride back to Grande Terre, Christophe and Delphine would be unable to refrain themselves from enthusing.

Meanwhile Alexandria settled back into her solitary life.

Was it better? Or was the whole situation another mixed bag? Having the whole island to herself was a joy, one which she had difficulty expressing in words sometimes. Of an evening, sitting on her lawn, replete with good simple food, watching the sun go down, finishing the wine, she could sometimes imagine that she was the happiest woman in the world. No problems, no arguments, no-one, not even a family member, to come along and disturb her peace. Her existence was just so thoroughly simple.

She had learned to appreciate that now. But it might not be quite so straightforward for all westerners. Whatever they might say, no matter what she herself might have said before, was it possible to jettison completely all the learned sophistication?

In other words, was it really possible to go backwards, to become more primitive, almost to regress? Or would all that western sophistication one day come back home to roost, tugging at the sleeve, trying to lure back both the heart and the mind?

As a prime example, had not the Australian after more than twenty years, his French partner too after more than ten, finally succumbed to the allure represented by 21st-century affluent society?

Okay, everyone was different. But if they had so fully espoused such a primitive life, only to eventually forsake it for a return to a more conventional one, what hope was there for the rest? In time would she, Alexandria, succumb the same? She could not know. Only time would tell. But just for now her whole being - body, mind, heart and soul - seemed satisfied, fulfilled.

She had no reason to believe that the man on the tiller would start touting around for other potential visitors.

He was not the sort somehow. She felt that she knew him, could trust him. Sure, he had a living to make like everyone else, a family to support, but at no point had he showed himself to be greedy.

No doubt many of the locals, as tourism over the years

increased, became exactly that. If you looked around, it was the way the world. In the end, as tourism arrived, few locals could resist the temptation to jump on the bandwagon.

Some even went further - to squeeze every last drop out of it that they could. One suspected that most of them, whilst becoming materially richer, were also sacrificing a traditional way of life. It seemed a heavy price. The question posed itself - were they all aware, as well as what they were gaining, of what they were losing?

Chapter Nineteen

After a few months, once again on his occasional visit, the man on the tiller arrived accompanied.

It was a couple from Argentina, somewhat younger than the French couple had been. Once again the man on the tiller seemed to recommend them. Alexandria explained her terms. They were acceptable.

After the unloading of all the provisions, the couple's as well as Alexandria's, she picked up a container of fresh water, put it on her back and proceeded to lead them through the forest. They took their time. It brought back memories to her - of the first time that she had ventured along this path.

What sense of wonder it had inspired in her back then! Maybe now it was inspiring the same sense of wonder in this new pair. She showed them the treehouse, told them where to find the beach hut, not so very much further on. They looked satisfied. She explained one or two things again, then duly took her leave.

Once again she felt a little ambivalent.

There was a bit of company to be had, plus no reason to believe that it would be any less amenable this time than the last. Okay, this time there was a bit of a language difficulty but so far that had not proved too much of a problem. They all seemed to understand fairly well. If they all spoke reasonably slowly - she in French, they in Spanish - they all seemed to get the gist pretty easily. In fact, it proved quite fun. Now that everything was settled, there was no reason why, in the course of their stay, they should not have further conversation together.

But yes, it was different somehow. The feel was different. When she had the island to herself, she felt completely uninhibited. She could sing or shout, do exactly what she liked, exactly when she liked. And yes, she could even decide whether to wear clothes or not.

Somehow now she did not feel quite so free, could not be quite so uninhibited. Her guests might be living all of two kilometres away, with no intention of calling on her more than the agreed once per day at noon. Nevertheless, she was conscious of them all the time, conscious of their presence. It seemed both positive and negative, all at the same time.

On the other hand, it was only for a couple of weeks. There were fifty more in the year where she could go back to doing exactly as she liked. One day that might prove to be a luxury which no longer appealed so much. Who knew? She might wind up missing them after they had gone.

She had with Delphine and Christophe. There she had wound up thinking more about them after they had gone than while they were there. When she saw them off, seeing the little boat chugging away, she seemed to be missing them already. She continued watching it as it faded into the distance, in the end becoming just a little speck on the ocean. Nor did she have any means of keeping in touch with them. But that was her choice. She decided to stick with it.

Before they left, the Argentinian couple also shared a last-evening meal with her.

They were anxious to leave her with a kind of parting gift. Begonia began.

"Do you know, Alexandria? You have made us want to change direction in life. When we eventually return to Argentina, we are planning to make radical changes. We'll probably sell up where we are living now and move out into the country, maybe somewhere quite remote. We will find an old house to renovate or maybe even build a new one ourselves. We'll grow crops, plant fruit trees and in general live a more natural life. There are beautiful parts of Argentina, with a favourable climate, and now we aim to take advantage of that, to live a more natural way."

Guillermo took it up.

"Our thinking has not just been changed by the beauty of your island, more by yourself, the way you live, the way you are. You're not just dreaming the dream. You're living it. And it seems to ooze out of your every pore. You are naturally you at all times. No act, no pretence, no falseness. You even show it when you are disappointed, though it be rare. As you yourself said, there is so much falseness and pretence in the world. We, like you, have had our fill of it. When we return to Argentina, we intend to be more ourselves too - with friends, with family, with everyone. They can take us or leave us, but from now on we will be true to our natures, one hundred percent. And it's all thanks to you, dear Alexandria."

Once again they left behind a permanent invitation to visit, which all parties knew was unlikely to be fulfilled. But as they sailed away, they were leaving behind something quite as valuable, another fond memory for her to enjoy during the coming days, weeks, months of solitude.

So if she were honest with herself, Alexandria would have to admit to herself that after this latest departure she had mixed feelings.

It was not just unique to her and to her situation. It was more part of the human condition - that we enjoyed good company but at the same time sought periods without any. That was almost the dilemma in life, for some at least, all part of the self-contradictions. Alexandria was just as susceptible as anyone else.

In a sense, now she had less choice about it. Or rather, she had already exercised her choice, even in a rather dramatic way. There was no halfway house out here. It was not even like that country which she knew so well - France - where you could enjoy the benefits, the peace, of the countryside, in the knowledge that you could just jump in the car and within, say, half an hour, be in a large village or a small town, with shops, bars, even a cinema.

Thinking about it now, that was exactly what she could have had. She knew the country well, spoke the language, liked the people. In fact, thousands of her fellow countrymen did exactly that - either early in life or more likely later - decamped across the English Channel, bought a piece of land bigger than an English garden, renovated the house and lived happily ever after, or not, as the case may be.

Somehow, looking back, that had never been a serious consideration. She was not part enough of that mainstream. That was too much like living within the normal world. Okay, it was a radical enough move for most, even daring, bold.

But for her somehow, it would not have been extreme enough. When your dreams were all broken, a more extreme solution was needed. There had to be a real turning of the back. And now, like it or not, she had to live with it. Most days, like it she did.

Chapter Twenty

It was another nine months before the man on the tiller brought another visitor over.

He looked a little hesitant as he climbed up on to the jetty. The visitor stayed put for the time being, sitting in the prow of the boat. This visit, clearly, was not exactly a fait accompli. In fact, Alexandria was already thinking.

'Has he taken leave of his senses or something? What on earth is he doing, bringing over a single man? I know that we've never discussed it as such, not explicitly. But I took it to be understood that he would only bring couples over. Or maybe two women together, as they often travel nowadays. After all, this is an island, a small one, for goodness sake! Apart from the obvious danger, what if we don't get along? With a couple, two people, that matters less. They have their own self-sufficiency. This situation will be different. It's too loaded.'

The visitor was saying nothing, just staying put. Looking at him, he seemed naturally quiet anyway. Was that a good or a bad thing? Did we not all know what people said about the quiet ones? On the other hand, was it fair to judge him like that? Alexandria decided to hear the man on the tiller out.

"He's an interesting fellow, originally from the Auvergne, a small department called the Cantal. I've known him for some time. He has been living in Nouméa. He used to be an academic, lecturing on botany, with particular reference to the southern hemisphere. I believe that at first he took a sabbatical, a year off, although right from the outset, from what he was telling me, he was never certain to return to his post. It was left a bit open. If necessary his replacement could continue. I think that eventually simple events decided it. Now he works casually at the market in the capital, just to keep body and soul together, I suppose. And yet, from time to time he still feels that yen to go off and do some fieldwork, to study plants and, I guess, also the creatures and birds, particularly in this part of the Pacific, where some species are rare and currently under threat. When I told him about your island, he very nearly pleaded with me to bring him over. He says that he'll be no trouble at all. He knows how to survive now in these outlying primitive regions. He'll pay your going rate but ask for virtually nothing in return."

Alexandria's mind was taking it all in. All the time she was looking at the seated man but could glean nothing from his countenance. He did not look aggressive, more the contrary. All the time a little smile seemed to be playing about his lips. Already he seemed to be so happy to be out here. Finally it was time for her to speak.

"You put me in an invidious position, you know, Émile. I thought that you would know better. You must see how awkward this is. How long does he want to stay?"

"A month."

"A month! What are you thinking? What if it doesn't work out? A month's an awfully long time. Would you be prepared to come back over early, say if he rang to ask you?"

"He doesn't have a phone."

Alexandria bit her lip and stopped herself from voicing the words which easily came to her mind, at least one of them a swearword, one which hitherto she had only used when speaking to herself.

It must be clear to everyone that what the Frenchman had brought in his puny bags would not even come close to lasting him for a month. What about her resolve? What about her pact with herself? Had she not studiously avoided being drawn into arguments all her life?

And yet here she was now, on her idyllic Pacific island, its peace having been momentarily disturbed, finding herself at odds with the only man in the vicinity who she thought she could trust, arguing the toss with him, on the verge of getting heated, very heated. She took a long breath and tried to calm her voice.

"Very well, Émile. He's here now and I can see that he's brought a few provisions with him, although I doubt if they'll last him for long. But if, as you say, he is resourceful and knows how to look after himself out in these primitive jungle places, then I guess that he'll survive all right. But this is the first and last time, Émile. I'm almost inclined to put an embargo on the whole visiting thing altogether. You really have tried my patience this time. Just make sure that it doesn't happen again!"

Nothing further was said.

She left the two men to it, to unload the boat, to take her provisions inside, while the visitor's remained outside, keeping company with his small rucksack. Meanwhile she loaded on her back a container of fresh water. The man on the tiller was still looking rather sheepish as he said his goodbyes, got back into the little boat and started up the outboard motor.

"See you in a month's time then!"

She did not reply but simply turned her back and set off for the gate at the end of the garden, the one leading into the forest. It seemed that she had little time just now for the niceties of conversation.

"Suivez-moi, Monsieur!"

The man had little alternative but to follow.

Chapter Twenty-One

So it could not exactly be said that things were getting off on the right foot.

More the contrary - what an inauspicious beginning to this latest visit! Still she was running it through her mind as to whether she would indeed go through with her threat and make it the last. Suddenly visits from outside seemed more trouble than they were worth. Had she not, after all, sought a refuge from that very outside world? In the end, was she not simply doing herself a great disservice by allowing it back in again?

Just look what it brought! - Just trouble! Conflict and argument! She did not owe the outside world anything. When she left it, they were quits. She did not need it any more. She certainly did not need the aggro. No, she was decided already. When the man on the tiller appeared in a month's time, she would tell him straight -

'No more, Émile! In future you can take your inquisitive visitors to some other island to bother some other poor soul!'

She hated this.

Walking through the forest in single file, not exchanging a single word - she hated it. She was not even sure if the man was keeping up with her. She was hastening her step more than usual, just wanting to get the whole thing over and done with. He, on the other hand, was walking more and more slowly, just looking all around him - at the vegetation, at all the little creatures, listening to the birds, watching their antics. If he slowed down any further, he would stop.

He did. He did that very thing - just stopped. He even put his bags down, so that he could concentrate more. She would not have noticed, except that she heard him, just, above the jungle buzz, almost in a whisper.

"Quelle beauté!"

It made her head swivel round. He was already a full 50 metres behind. She sighed with impatience and was just about to call out to him to get a move on - 'Dépêchez-vous!' - but he beat her to it again, this time more loudly, so that she definitely would hear.

"Vraiment! Quelle beauté! En réalité, Mademoiselle, vous habitez dans un véritable paradis!"

She did not respond but just looked back at him, hard. A boyish grin spread across his whole face. He was clearly younger than her by a good few years. Just now, especially with her frowning, he looked half her age.

She saw the grin and suddenly could not find it in her heart to be too severe with him. Plus, after all, where was the hurry? It was only her, being petulant. Was not even that absolutely ridiculous? She had not come to live out here, in his words, in her true paradise, only to give vent to her own petulance.

She thought that that belonged to the past, belonged to the old Alexandria, had been drowned somehow on the passage out here. Apparently not! Apparently it still lay hidden inside her, still ready to raise its ugly head, even, it seemed, at the slightest excuse. Yes, it was ridiculous. She would have to school it, somehow eliminate it. But not today. She was not in the mood. In fact, she was still in a bad one.

Eventually - they must be making all of one kilometre per hour - they arrived at the clearing.

The man immediately noticed the treehouse. Once again he was looking up at it in boyish wonder. He needed no invitation. He set his bags down and proceeded to climb up the rickety wooden ladder. At this point Alexandria was just hoping that it would bear his weight. Fortunately it did. She did not accompany him. He could look around on his own. She would wait, patiently. Or impatiently.

In the event she had to be patient. What was he finding to do up there? Even she, on first discovering the treehouse a few years earlier, intrigued as she was, had not taken this long. What was there to look at up there, for goodness sake? Then she noticed - that as well as looking at the interior, he was also gazing at the exterior, looking through the open windows at the surrounding trees and all their inhabitants. In fact, she realised that, unless she intervened somehow, she would never prise him away.

"Monsieur! I've still got to show you the beach hut."

He smiled down at her.

"No, there is no need, Mademoiselle. I have found my happiness here. This treehouse will do me perfectly. I'll go exploring on my own later and I'm sure that I will find the seashore and the beach hut without too much trouble. But thank you so much for your hospitality. You are an angel, Mademoiselle, and therefore deserve to live in such a paradise."

It left her speechless, almost puzzled.

Yes, had she not come across it so many times before, particularly during her many travels through France? - this Gallic charm, laid on not lightly but heavily? She had never fallen for it before. She had always seen through it, sort of heard through it. She knew the game and was determined not to participate in it. Count her out!

But here, now, his words sounded so sincere. Or rather they sounded so sincerely expressed. No, it did not sound put on, said to impress. His words were heartfelt. She could feel it. Just now they were silencing her, stopping her from fighting back, stopping her from calling out -

'Come off it, you sweet-talking Frenchman! I've heard it all before! More through good luck than anything, you've managed to wheedle your way on to my precious little island. So just be thankful for that! In other words, don't overcook it! Don't try to gild the lily! Just be grateful that you've got a basic rustic shack halfway up a tree, your home for a month! And don't come bothering me! I won't welcome it!'

No, she kept her silence. He did not keep his. He finally came back down the ladder to rejoin her.

"You must allow me to pay you in advance. In fact, let me pay you a bit extra - for all the fruit, water etc, maybe a few vegetables. If I may, if they're growing outside your garden, sort of in the wild, I'll help myself. If I do - if you let me pay a bit more - then I will feel better about gathering all this lovely produce growing round about. I always knew that I would not be able to carry a full month's provisions but would have to supplement it by what I found in the wild. I think that I might just be able to last out, see myself through. It's a happy solution, isn't it?"

Still she could not find any reply. He handed over the banknotes. She watched as he counted them out. Yes, he was paying her for a full thirty nights, plus 25% extra. She wanted to protest but instead just found herself reaching her hand out and taking the bills offered. She did not even say 'Thank-you'.

He did not seem to need her thanks. Already he had picked up one bag and was ascending the ladder again. He seemed keen to get himself installed. In short time everything was up aloft, including the water. In no time at all the bed was draped with a light sheet-sleeping bag. He certainly seemed to know how to make himself at home.

It suddenly seemed as if she were surplus to requirements.

She turned to go. The words came to her mind - 'If you need anything, don't hesitate … … !' - but once again she could not voice them. Or rather, she deliberately stopped herself. No, she would leave him to it, just remind him that this, the north shore, was the part of the island which he should stick to. He grinned in reply, as if to say -

'What more could I wish for? Without your knowing it, you have just made an old man, rather still a youngish man, very happy.'

Chapter Twenty-Two

For the rest of the first week she saw neither hide nor hair of him.

That was curious. At the very least she expected him to appear once a day, or at the very least once every two days, if only to collect a new supply of fresh water. But no, she had seen no sign of him whatsoever. It seemed as if he really were keeping to the letter of her law, staying on his patch, not risking even one step outside.

But how was he surviving? Without fresh water? Okay, he had made it pretty clear that he would be helping himself to as much fruit as he could find. And yes, of course, pretty well all fruit contained moisture, plenty of it, some more than others.

Nevertheless, she doubted if anyone, especially in this climate, could stay healthily hydrated on just consuming fruit. Thinking about it, she judged it unlikely. What was going on? She even began to feel a little concerned, even worried.

She immediately set off.

She just remembered in time. Just as house removals apprentices learned on day one - never to enter or leave a house empty-handed but always to make the journey worthwhile, carrying something - so she, before leaving, fetched up a container of fresh water.

Whatever his circumstances, no matter how much he might be secreting away unbeknown to her, a little bit extra would never go amiss, might save him a visit. In any case, she always liked to feel useful. If he were, as she suspected, desperately short of drinking water, perhaps parched and half-dying somewhere, did it not make sense to take him some? Soon she had the container on her back.

Arriving at the clearing by the treehouse, she saw no sign of him. But there was no point in taking the water any further. In fact, she would feel quite relieved to get it off her back. She decided not to take it up the ladder - too risky for her. She would leave it under the tree, in the shade. He would not fail to come across it later. She was sure that, whatever, it would not be for him an unwelcome sight.

She ascended the rickety contraption. His things were all still there. But he could be anywhere. It was only a small island - 5.6 km² - but with the dense vegetation, it would be like looking for a needle in a haystack. In fact, someone who was determined not to be found could stay undiscovered for weeks, maybe longer.

Not that she had any reason to believe that he wanted to go into hiding or anything. More likely he was exploring, trekking through the jungle, not on the well trodden paths but making his own way, hacking his way through with a machete, just like the natives, half wishing he were one, at least temporarily living like one.

From what little she knew of him, that seemed to be his objective in life. Put it like this - looking at him, one would immediately guess that he had lost all other ambition, any real ambition.

Well, she had come this far, so she might just as well complete the loop, even if it were a long shot.

She continued along the path, still heading north. She slowed down now. Even so, it was not long before she saw the break in the trees ahead and the blue beyond. All at once she could hear the ocean, hear the waves lapping the shore. Never was it a disagreeable sound somehow, more one which was comforting, reassuring.

Having got this far, she might even spend a little time up here for a change, a change of beach, a change of orientation. She dipped her feet in the water. It felt so good. After all, it was her beach hut, her beach. She could still do what she liked. Bugger him! Wherever he was! Wherever he might be!

She found him outside the beach hut, just sitting there, just gazing out to sea.

As she approached, he did not even avert his eyes, look in her direction. He just seemed to sense her presence.

"Bonjour, Mademoiselle."

"Bonjour, Monsieur."

It seemed totally incoherent, even completely absurd - such formality, out here. Anyone hearing but not seeing might presume that they were investor and stockbroker, meeting for the first time at 'La Bourse', the stock exchange in Paris. Maybe even there there would be less formality.

She did not even know his name. He only knew hers from the man on the tiller. And yet here they were, as if shipwrecked together on a desert island, addressing each other as if they were figuring together in some upper-middle-class nineteenth century novel. Yes, it was truly absurd. And yet it seemed to be no laughing matter.

Or was it? As he turned towards her, his face broke out into his customary smile. Yes, he seemed pleased to see her, but then he seemed pleased at everything. At any rate, he certainly did not seem displeased to see her. He invited her to sit down on the chair next to his. She accepted. They sat in silence for a few minutes, both just watching the ocean.

"How have you been?"

Her voice sounded quiet, calm.

"Ça va. Everything is all right. In fact, everything is great. How about you?"

"I thought I might have seen you before now. Do you come up to the house during the night, to draw water, I mean, so as not to disturb me? But that's not necessary, you know. I told you that I expect you to call round once per day. If you make it around noontime, I'll know to expect you. At the same time, I'll be assured that the rest of the time I won't be disturbed. That's how it has worked before and worked pretty well."

He thought a moment before replying.

"No, I don't come up to the house, not even at night. I wouldn't do that anyway, not without asking first. It might spook you if you heard a noise outside, an unfamiliar one. No, I haven't been up for any water."

He paused again. She did not say anything by way of reply but seemed to expect further explanation.

"I've been using desalination tablets. I brought a supply over with me, just in case. In fact, I take them with me wherever I go. You just never know. It may sound like a small detail, one easily overlooked, but if you think about it, they could in certain circumstances be a bit of a lifesaver. For instance, supposing Émile's little boat broke down halfway across! I know that we could probably row somewhere, either to here or back to Grande Terre. But suppose the wind were blowing a gale or the currents were stronger than usual. Put it like this - we might not make landfall for a day or two, maybe longer. In such circumstances, having a few desalination tablets could make all the difference, not just to the comfort of the situation but maybe even to survival. Out here the sun is fairly merciless and one easily gets dehydrated. Stuck in the middle of an expanse of saltwater, those tablets could be a lifesaver."

It was her turn to pause before replying.

"So that's what you've been doing - taking water from the ocean and making it drinkable with tablets?"

He nodded but said nothing.

"What's it like? I mean, the purified drinking water? How does it taste?"

This time he did not hesitate.

"Something horrible!"

They both laughed.

Maybe it was the way that he said it, really getting his throat around that double 'rr'. It just seemed to tickle them, both at the same time. Plus, the thought of it - him stuck out here on the north coast, reluctantly sticking a desalination tablet in a beaker of lukewarm saltwater, waiting for it to perform its dubious magic, knowing that in a few minutes' time he would be having to force down a life-saving but horrible-tasting liquid, worse than any nasty-tasting medicine, his face screwing up at the mere thought of it.

The looked at each other and both burst into laughter again. Just like the formality between them, it was so absurd. Okay, just for now they were living on what was rightly termed a primitive little island. But the fact of the matter was that she had at her fingertips pretty well all modern amenities. In particular, she had an inextinguishable supply of electricity through solar power.

In addition, she had a modern desalination plant which had produced ample water for a couple before, even in excess. Just now she was only using a fraction of it. At the same time he was scrambling about on the north shore, half-poisoning himself to death, certainly putting himself through unnecessary discomfort. Yes, it was absurd. No wonder they were both laughing uncontrollably! Finally she was able to string a few words together.

"Écoutez, Monsieur!"

Even that set them off laughing again, without their knowing why. Once again it took her a minute or two to recompose herself.

"Now listen, Monsieur! I want you to promise me something - that you will stop using these damned desalination tablets and come up to the house and collect fresh water, as agreed, will you? Will you do that for me? Please?"

It looked as if he were not sure whether to burst out laughing again. In the absence of a reply from him, she had a further threat to make.

"Because if you don't, if you continue to play this ridiculous little pantomime, then I will come out to you in the dead of night. Somehow I'll find and steal your little supply of tablets, go straight up to the north shore and sling them as far as I can, out into the waves. It'll be goodbye to your damned desalination tablets. Then you will have no choice, none whatsoever. Then I'll have you where I want you. Your resistance will be finished."

Still he said nothing, just smiled. Then he did and said something extraordinary. He reached across his left arm, lowered it and with his left hand squeezed hard her bare right knee.

"Mademoiselle Alexandria, when first I clapped eyes on you, on your jetty just a few days ago, I knew right away that you were the kindest of people."

Chapter Twenty-Three

She thought about it afterwards, even repeating to herself his words, verbatim.

How could he say such a thing? He had first known her at her very worst, worse than she had been most times back in her homeland. Dealing with the man on the tiller on the jetty, as they arrived, she had been an absolute cow!

So how could this Frenchman, unless he were after all just oozing false Gallic charm, how could he claim now to have seen back then, at her ugliest, that she was not just kind but of the kindest?

It did not add up. And yet, when she had looked at him, looked into his eyes, once again she had seen that unmistakable sincerity. No, he was not lying. No, he was not even putting on the charm. He was speaking the truth, from the heart, from his heart.

It continued to prey on her mind.

Who was he really? - this self-contradictory man from the wild and wonderful Cantal? But were we not all, in a sense, self-contradictory? Was not she, Alexandria, a prime example? Sometimes she did not even recognise herself, so what hope had anyone else? Plus, was it so amazing that someone else, someone who was probably more perceptive than most, had seen beneath the surface, even when she was putting on her worst act?

But who was he? This enigma of a man? Was he as he appeared - young for his age, a bit naïve, even playful? Or, on the other hand, almost at the other extreme, was he mature for his years, wiser than most, even a little philosopher? The jury was out. But still he continued to intrigue her. For the rest of the day she could not get him off her mind.

Round about noon on the following day she saw him come through the garden gate.

Even she gave a bit of a smile this time. In fact, she seemed genuinely pleased to see him.

"I guess that you've come for the water. Even you can be obedient sometimes, Monsieur. I've got a container ready for you. But stay a while if you like. Around this time I often take a noontime drink. Would you like to join me? What's your preference? Beer or wine?"

He was moving so slowly. And his love of life seemed to be reflected all the time by the pleasant expression on his face.

"Whatever you're having. I'll have the same as you. As you know, I'm not difficult to please."

He always seemed to express himself in this light, almost ironic way, not untypical of the French. A few minutes later she returned to the table carrying two tinnies and two glasses.

"How are you finding the north shore?"

"Perfect!"

"Have you got everything you need? I'm sure you'll have noticed that actually this place, the house and gardens, is pretty well appointed, in fact lacks for nothing. There are loads of vegetables growing. There's a whole set of tools and garden implements. If you want to borrow any or to take some of the produce, don't hesitate. You don't even need to ask me."

"You're very kind, Alexandria. I might well take you up on that offer. I do want to take some samples back with me when I go back to the main island. I still carry on some research, if admittedly in a somewhat more amateur way nowadays. I haven't lost my passion for things that grow. It was just the context of work which in the end proved less than satisfactory. That's so often the case, isn't it? You can love what you do, your work, the real work - as an actor, as a sportsman, as an academic. It's just all the rest, all the paraphernalia that goes with it in the form of bureaucracy and politics. That's what ruined it in the end for me. One starts off doing something one loves. Then later on one only finds constraints, when one is hankering after freedom. Freedom has become in such short supply now, such that it can often present you with a stark choice - pursue the career you always wanted in a formal way or choose a less conventional option. Play the game or stay true to yourself. It can be a tough choice sometimes. In the end, for me it wasn't. It was a choice which almost made itself. And then afterwards I never had cause to regret it, even if I only have two shirts to my back and I'm constantly having to repair my moccasins. But at least I have freedom in the heart now."

She could see it. It sort of shone out of him, as if his face were like a little ray of sunshine. There was nearly always a curl about his lip. Above all his eyes shone. She looked at him now and almost felt, despite the extreme poverty in which he seemed to live, envious. She went and fetched another couple of tinnies.

"Are you sure?" he asked. "Do you need to be getting on with something?"

"No, I only work in the mornings. In the afternoons I watch the ocean. And dream."

"One day, out here, are you going to write your memoirs?"

"No, I'm just a sentimental old fool, that's all. When I was young, I had these childish notions - about love and passion. I really believed in it, all that romantic nonsense. During my teenage years, instead of going to watch modern films, I used to try and seek out the old ones, many in black-and-white, like 'Dangerous Moonlight' or 'Brief Encounter'. I read Jane Austen, Charlotte Brontë, read them over and over again. I had to keep it to myself, of course. This was the 1980s, after all. Few of my girlfriends were romantic and if from time to time they did find out what I had been watching or reading, then of course they would take the mickey out of me something rotten. I just had to try and take it on the chin. But I knew that I was different. I also knew that it was something which I would not grow out of. And I didn't."

"Sometimes we know the real truths so early in life, when we're really young."

"And then as I entered my adult years, I looked all around me.

Everyone was pairing up. Some were getting married, including most of my girlfriends. But I often wondered for what reasons. No, of course, I'm not saying that they didn't marry for love, that their men were not marrying them for love either. But it seemed a very mixed picture. Shall we just say that quite often practical considerations seemed to be at the forefront? Parents were always talking about making a good match. It all seemed to be about complementing each other, meeting each other's mutual needs. Even the weddings had to be meticulously planned, almost like a military campaign. And I was left wondering - where was the romance in all this? Answer - it had all been squeezed out."

"We live in a cynical, materialist world now."

"And then later on, complacency would set in. Put it like this - if, as I'm sure was true, there was love in the first place, few couples seemed to look after it. Worse than that, they seemed to neglect it, to just assume that it would go on living without being fed. That's what I was seeing all around me. But I did not want that, not for myself. I wanted something better, the real thing, something which would last. Funnily enough, it wouldn't have to last all life long, say sixty years. Even I'm a bit of a realist and know that that must be a bit of tough act. I would have gladly settled for a relationship half that long, provided that the love was kept alive, surfaced every day, was at the heart of the relationship, of the life together. I wanted love to remain real, not become in time, almost inevitably, a distant memory."

Julien smiled an understanding smile.

Chapter Twenty-Four

The following noontime she had lunch waiting for him.

It was nothing grand, just one of her usual mixed salads. Making the French vinaigrette sauce, she had smiled to herself, wondering what he would make of it, whether he would approve. There were also eggs and some local cheese. On seeing the table laid out, he laughed.

"I don't know whether to call you predictable or unpredictable, Alexandria. But I do like the way that you don't ask first. You just do it."

"I hope that it's not too early for you. In fact we can leave it for another half an hour or so, even longer. It's not as if it's going to go cold. In any case, it will be nice to have a drink before. Where would a Frenchman be without his 'apéritif'? In fact, I've been in situations in France where the apéritif has lasted longer than the following meal. And that's saying something!"

He could believe her. Soon he was pouring beer into two tall glasses. When three quarters of an hour later they set about eating, she opened a bottle of red wine and poured two glasses. They chatted some more. She could not remember having had a more pleasant lunch. Perhaps he might have said the same. But there was still half the wine to finish.

"Did you never marry either, Julien?"

It was a simple enough question, although he seemed to hesitate to answer.

"No, I never went through a marriage ceremony. But I did once have what is known as a long-term relationship. I even have a daughter. It started off well enough, as always. We both had good careers, had together a good standard of living. The child was not planned, was an accident, if you like. I was not displeased but she, my partner, was, very. Nevertheless, she could not bring herself to seek a termination and I would not have agreed to it anyway. When the baby was born, I was delighted and I hoped by this time that my partner would be, if not quite so much. But that seemed to be when the problems started. Needless to say, she had to give up work, at least temporarily. In fact, we agreed that she wouldn't resume her career for five years, when the child would start school. I thought that she might get to quite like a more leisurely, less hectic lifestyle, not working for a few years, especially if she knew that it would one day come to an end and she could get back to her career as an anaesthetist. But she never really settled into life as housewife/mother."

"I've often wondered what I would have been like at that."

"Plus, it had the effect that she became even more ambitious for me. She wanted me to increase my efforts to get up the ladder, so to speak. I think that she had this idea of my becoming one day Professor of Botany at the Sorbonne. She wanted me to start courting all the senior academics, wanted me to write papers and circulate them, to go on lecture tours. If I had followed up all her suggestions I would have literally doubled my workload with no time at all for anything outside work. But that was not how I viewed life. In any case, I had a daughter now. If anything, she was becoming more important than work. Increasingly I found myself wanting to spend more and more time with her. Far from my wanting to become more ambitious, I almost wanted my work to take second stage. Instead of doing the maximum, I wanted to do the minimum. To me it was all about balance. But it was something on which we could not see eye-to-eye."

"As you say, balance in these things is all-important."

"Things really started to go downhill. We only stayed together because of the child, I'm sure of it. But even that is not good, not really a good enough reason for staying together. Even a young child will inevitably start to pick up on things around it, I mean will become aware of not being part of a wholly loving household. I just did my best, as she got older, to try to disguise it all, so that she did not notice. But I don't know if I succeeded."

He paused, reflecting for a moment, before continuing.

"Anyway, to cut a long story short, soon after Mélodie's fifth birthday we split up. My partner resumed her career as anaesthetist. I took custody of Mélodie. There was no fight over that, no battle through the courts. My partner probably would have suggested it if I hadn't. I think that she was glad to be rid of the responsibility, the daily caring. She called round at my place from time to time, even took Mélodie out a bit. But I soon noticed that the visits were becoming more and more infrequent. Eventually they stopped. I, on the other hand, didn't mind at all. In a way the whole thing had worked in my favour. I now had no choice but to spend tons of time with Mélodie. She was my sole responsibility. It gave me even more incentive to reduce my responsibilities at work. I now had a first class pretext to go to my superiors at the University of Lyon and ask for time off, to work fewer hours. No, this was no way to realise a grand ambition, but that had never been mine, only my partner's. Now I was free of it, as well as being free of her."

"It's funny how these things work out sometimes."

"And I can honestly say that we were a happy little household. Somehow the light returned. Things weren't so heavy. I got my sense of humour back. We could joke about nearly anything, the two of us, even about little disasters, even about spilt milk. And even though I say it myself, I think it was then that Mélodie started to blossom. She was carefree, I could see it. She felt secure, as never before. At school she became outgoing. I knew that the teachers were pleased with her, with her enthusiasm and energy. She started taking piano lessons and loved it. At the same time, unprompted by me, she started to take interest in my work. She began to draw or paint some of the plants and flowers I collected. She asked me about them, wanting to know more. Of course, it was a delight for me, a complete bonus. I took great pleasure in explaining all that I thought that she could understand. Like me she seemed to have an instinct for it. Put it like this - if in the end her mother and I had not proved to be such a good match, the daughter and I were proving to be a very good match indeed, near perfect."

"That must have been a blessing. But I'm sure you earned it."

"I'm not going to say that we had no problems at all. All families do. But I think that we had fewer than most. Even as she entered adolescence, she did not become rebellious or difficult. In fact, in a curious way, she became more supportive. She seemed to recognise that it wasn't a hundred percent easy, life as a single parent, trying to balance work with home life, raising a child. She seemed to know all that instinctively. She was doing more and more in the home - cleaning, doing the washing, doing the cooking. At the same time she was undemanding. In fact, it was incredible. I knew all her friends, saw how different they were. Talk about self-centred! Talk about Me! Me! Me! Put it like this - I don't think that many of them were falling over themselves to do the household chores at home. More it was a case of - 'Take me here! Take me there! Can I have that for my birthday? That for Christmas? That for no special occasion?' Mélodie was the opposite. I can honestly say that she has brought me nothing but undiluted joy. How many parents can say that? I'll leave you to answer."

"As a non-parent, I'm sure you're right."

"It was when it was coming to the end of her school career. She obtained a place at the University of Aix-en-Provence, in the Art faculty, for the following autumn. I immediately applied to take a sabbatical, a year off. I felt that I needed it. Okay, I've just painted what was indeed a peaceful home life. But the work situation was not always so peaceful. There were professional jealousies. There's always red tape. Suddenly I'd had a bellyful. And with Mélodie's imminent departure, it seemed the perfect opportunity to take a bit of time off, to recharge my batteries, so to speak. Plus, I had always wanted to travel, particularly within the southern hemisphere. That had not been possible, of course, during the previous years. Now there opened up the opportunity. I had my eye on New Caledonia. I put in the application to the head of department. It was all agreed in remarkably short time and with remarkably little difficulty.

Maybe they, my university, welcomed a break from me too. Put it like this - I hadn't always been the most co-operative member of staff, the most compliant. It was even they, my employers, who suggested the rider - 'Okay, Julien, we'll make the sabbatical for a year but should you wish to extend it, it might be possible. We would sound out your replacement, to see if they were prepared to continue.' That was two and a half years ago and I still haven't returned. And if I'm honest with myself, I don't suppose that I have any intention of doing so. I might be on my uppers but I have found a contentment out here in the peaceful Pacific which it's almost impossible to find in western Europe, in France, even out in the countryside. Plus, the bonus is that Mélodie comes out to visit me every year, in fact spends the whole of the summer vacation here. She loves it too, of course. In fact, when in six months' time she graduates, she is threatening to come out for a whole year. She says that she'll help me out at the market, earning a pittance. She won't mind that. She'll be happy too, having two shirts to her back and permanently repaired moccasins. It would just be something else for us to laugh about. But needless to say, I can't wait. When she arrives I will truly be the happiest of men."

Alexandria did not need any convincing.

Chapter Twenty-Five

Another lunchtime they got talking again.

"So it's a long time since you split up with Mélodie's mother, I guess about fifteen years. But you must have had other loves since. Put it like this - it would be rather unusual for a man not to have."

He grinned.

"But that's just you going making assumptions again, and not just about me but about men in general. You seem to imagine that we can't exist without having access to some sort of woman, wherever we go."

"But it's largely true, isn't it? I only use my eyes and ears. I bet that there aren't many men - only the very least attractive or the most timid - who seem to find themselves on their own for long periods. In fact, thinking about it, that probably doesn't even apply to the least attractive. Somehow they too manage to find a female to form their entourage. I know that it's dangerous to generalise. On the other hand, it's difficult not to entirely, when you're trying to make some sense of it all."

"But isn't the same true of most women? Isn't it roughly the same there, again with the exception of the least attractive and the most timid? Gone are the days of the one-man woman. No self-respecting fifty-year-old, finding herself abandoned by her children's father, now that they have all left home, is going to sit and mope alone at home for the rest of her days. She's going to get out there and, before you know where you are, she's going to have some smart man in tow. In fact, age and circumstance are pretty relevant. It's not so much now that the man leaves the little wife in order to run off with his younger secretary. It's more that the not so little wife decides that she's had enough of what might have been quite a bit of domestic drudgery and husband-pleasing and decides to strike out on her own, the finding of the new man occurring before or after and mattering little. The world has changed fast in our lifetime. No doubt it will keep on changing, including its social habits and norms. My parents belonged to the first generation who divorced. I belonged to the first generation who decided not to marry. Goodness knows what Mélodie's generation will become known as! Maybe it will be the first generation not to cohabit or to have children. Or the first to make adoption the norm, the western countries importing children from overpopulated areas all over the world, from poor countries not able to support them, to nurture them properly. I don't know. But there will be another key change, that is for sure. The world is not standing still. It never will. I'm not saying that that's a good or a bad thing. You will have your own views, I'm sure. I have mine. But whatever those views are, we won't be able to stop this crazy world of ours from keeping turning, from keeping changing, and not always for the better."

Alexandria did not appear to disagree.

The lunches together were becoming a habit and, if anything, were getting longer.

"Isn't it strange, I mean once you give up work, especially give up full-time work, how creative you become?"

It could have come from him but it came from her, although his reply did not perhaps chime one hundred percent.

"I suppose that it depends upon the person as well, not just the circumstances. I imagine that you have to have that creative gene implanted in you somewhere. But you're right that for many, the burden of full-time work keeps it suppressed, which is a pity."

"I can't really blow my own trumpet," she continued. "But I've discovered the pleasure of growing things, not only beautiful things like flowers but also things that nourish us bodily too, vegetables and fruits. It seems like giving Nature a helping hand, working in harmony with her. Whilst I don't play the piano much any more these days, I do find myself singing around the place. I listen to a lot of music. If I know the song, I sing along. I used to paint. I have no immediate plans to have painting materials brought over but I might give it a try in time. And who knows? One day I might, as you suggested, write my memoirs. It's too easy to think - that they'd be too dull to interest anyone else. Whilst it's probably true that I've had a relatively uneventful life compared to some, I still believe that I've had an interesting internal life, so to speak, one which might chime with others, even in this unromantic age of ours."

He was thinking, taking it all in. His reply indicated that he did not seem inclined to disagree.

"I've certainly found an immense freedom. In fact, I should say freedoms because there are several. Suddenly, released from the burden of full-time work, one is free, freed up, all one's energies and capacities, to spend them on other things, arguably more important things. One can interest oneself in anything, all the things one has been putting off. In contrast to you, I have started doing a little drawing. It was mainly when I first discovered that birds were so difficult to photograph. I tried and I tried but I could never get a really good shot. So I decided to try the next best thing - to draw them, quite simply, with pencil and paper. Later on I started trying to colour them in. I found using acrylics worked best because they don't run like watercolours and are less fiddly than oils. Don't get me wrong! I'm claiming to be no great talent. My first attempts were laughably poor, like a child's. It took me a while before I could get the hang of trying to turn two dimensions into three. Finally I discovered that it was all about the shading. Once I realised that, once I realised that all I really had to do was look more closely at Nature and simply copy her, all the different hues, light and dark, then Bingo! - even my drawings and paintings started to look a bit natural, like passable representations of what I had seen out in Nature, the beautiful creatures, now captured visually, more or less, and all my own work."

Alexandria understood his every word, wanting to put it her way.

"And the feeling is unique, isn't it? It's something which the world of work, so closely allied to the world of money, cannot give us. It's different, that feeling, rich and unique, irreplaceable, something which in fact no money can buy. It's probably something which most people don't get to experience their whole life long. In that sense we are the lucky ones. But it's only because we are the divorcees, so to speak. For whatever reasons, in whatever circumstances, we did find that little bit of courage - to divorce ourselves from work, from its world. We decided to live without it, without its oxygen. And then we found that we did not need it, that it was not oxygen. No, at worst it was carbon dioxide. At best it was just a sort of neutral nitrogen. Either way we needed neither. It was creativity which was the true oxygen, the true water of life. We could now overdose on that without danger. It was living without it that caused the perils, still did for the majority. They could be helped, if they would listen, like the couple I had from Argentina, your predecessors as visitors here. But the majority would not be open enough. The majority would just be keen to get back to the world of work after a pleasant interlude. Creativity would once again be crowded out by higher priorities, usually money."

"For most it's difficult to ignore," he replied. "As you say, you have to divorce it."

"But I wouldn't have missed this for the world. It has literally been like discovering a new one, one which nearly everyone, myself included, barely suspected existed, but one which we can go on to become intoxicated with. It's a good simile, because we could go on to become seriously addicted. But if there can be good addictions in life, this is one. And although it's habit-forming, dangerously so, the damage is little or non-existent. On the other hand, the benefits are huge and long-lasting. Even for those with an addictive personality, I'd recommend it wholeheartedly and without reserve and without concern for their well-being, knowing - that it could only benefit them. In fact, I'd say to anyone, working or otherwise - give it a try! There are no hidden dangers! Yes, it might become obsessive. But almost the greater danger is not to try it. There the risk is greater - of missing out on a whole new rich seam, like a coal seam hidden underground and likely to remain hidden there, undiscovered, never exploited, never touched, never used, never released. No, open it up without worry or thought of peril. You can only benefit and the benefits might be huge, rich and long-lasting. Get out your pick and shovel! Get out your hoe and trowel! Get out your pen and paper! Get out your pencils and sketching pad! Get out your canvas and paints! Get out your penny whistle or battered guitar! Get out your singing voice, even if it croaks or squeaks a bit! In a word, get anything out that works or shows even the smallest chance of working! And just see what happens! You have, literally, nothing to lose! But you have, literally, an awful lot to gain - a fortune, if not in material riches, just in heavenly ones, infinitely better!"

Julien was smiling, gazing at her in silence.

Chapter Twenty-Six

He got into the habit of calling round earlier in the mornings.

If he saw her working away at something, he would go over and give her a hand, perhaps even offer a word of advice. She had little experience of gardening or horticulture, was just trying to learn on the job. Even the vegetables were not familiar, nor the climatic conditions. He could help her there and did. She did not resent it but indeed welcomed it.

At noon they would knock off. They would both leave showering till later, he back on the north shore in the foamy brine, she in the freedom of the outdoors. She would prepare a quick lunch. They would chat about this and that, both about trivia and more serious matters, even personal issues. There seemed to be an ease growing between them. To put it a different way, there seemed to be a complete absence of distrust. It seemed that they could tell each other anything. Maybe it was something which neither of them had known for quite some time.

The setting seemed perfect. Having worked in the morning by the sweat of their brow, now taking a leisurely lunch, accompanied by cold beer and maybe even a glass or two of goodish wine, both of them now, it seemed, were on the same side. It all seemed to lead quite naturally to a most convivial atmosphere, one of ease, even trust.

If the conversation did at any time become a little too heavy, Julien could always be relied upon to prick the balloon in his inimitable sardonic manner. He would deliberately say something cynical. She knew that he did not mean it, in fact more likely believed the opposite. But it did keep it light. They could still giggle together and often did.

By the beginning of the fourth week he was making suggestions - on how she could improve things further.

There was still plenty of uncultivated land to convert. Not all the soil was rich but he knew which fruits and vegetables might thrive in such conditions. If she liked, when at the end of the month he returned to Grande Terre, he could give detailed instructions to the man on the tiller, get him to buy up some seeds and saplings, to bring over on his next trip, as part of her bimonthly provision delivery.

It was a useful and even welcome proposal, yet his words, very suddenly, filled her heart not with pleasure but gloom and of the darkest sort. It was the first time that he had ever mentioned the prospect of his returning to the main island, effectively of his leaving. It seemed to take her by surprise, as if it were completely unexpected. And yet, if she thought about it, it was the opposite - only to be expected. It was just that now it was suddenly brought home to her how unwelcome that prospect was.

She had got used to him by now. No, he was not part of the furniture. He never would be that, no matter what the circumstances. But she had got used to his presence. He had become part of her daily routine. He had become her conversation partner. He had, more or less, become her confidant. And now, in not much more than a few days' time, he was going to be gone. And she was going to miss him. In fact, that would be the understatement of her life.

He looked at her, evidently waiting for a response to his suggestion.

"But won't you need to show me? - I mean, how to prepare the ground, where best to locate everything, how deep to sow the seeds etc?"

He smiled.

"But I can do all that during my last few remaining days here. Plus, you're not an incapable woman, far from it. In fact, you've taken to this smallholding husbandry with quite some élan. Don't worry! You won't need me any more!"

Little did he know that those final half-dozen words first entered her mind through her ears but then went on to pierce her heart like darts.

They continued to talk over lunch.

Most times it did not even start with trivia. They sometimes discussed practical matters. But invariably they would share personal stuff. One day she was feeling nostalgic.

"When I was a child, I thought that everyone was sincere. I thought that everyone spoke the truth. In fact, I think that it was true within our household. And so, naturally, as a child, I thought that it would be the same everywhere. Of course, I now know - that it was an illusion, a naïve belief. Eventually even I had to grow out of it."

"It can be difficult growing up, especially if one did have an idyllic childhood."

"I can still remember the first time a dear friend of mine told me a lie. And I can still remember the first time I discovered that something I had taken to heart had not been meant by the person in earnest. Slowly and painfully I was seeing my idealised world fall apart, my cherished values going up in smoke, to be replaced by others not quite so noble - shallowness and superficiality. No, you could not rely on everyone's being sincere or even truthful. I was destined to be living within a world which was different from the one which I had hoped for. It was a world which I was destined to be at odds with. And so it proved."

"It is so sad to see a young person so disillusioned so early in life."

"I still tried to live within my own little bubble, so to speak, but the older I got, the more difficult it became. After all, you have to engage in life, engage with others, first at school, then at university, then in the world of work. It's a hard world out there. Most, it seems, are simply desperate to make as much money as they can, to acquire as many material possessions as they can. That seems to overshadow everything else, even to make them turn against themselves, against their better natures. In other words, they seem to sacrifice their finer feelings to adopt a more ruthless approach. But for what? Not to contribute to the good of humanity but just to enrich themselves personally, so that they can boast about how big their house is and how many cars it garages."

"That seems to be the trap into which most fall."

"It's one into which, if I'm honest, I fell myself. I got a first in mathematics at Durham University. Half the people wanted to push me towards an academic career, the other half towards one of the professions, probably accountancy. No-one seemed to give me a third option - like turning my back on the western world to go off and live in the middle of Nature. That took another thirty years for me to work out. I had to wait until I turned into a bitter old maid to prompt me to finally make the break, to turn my back on all the falseness and go somewhere else to discover and embrace purity and innocence. Looking back, it now seems a waste. But better late than never!"

"Never a truer word spoken, Mademoiselle!"

Chapter Twenty-Seven

She tried to make the best of the next few days but somehow the cloud would not lift entirely.

Their conversations did not seem to be so lively, so free-flowing. She still enjoyed them, but less. It seemed a bit of a waste, especially during his final week. But he was still there, they were still spending time together and they should, in a sense, celebrate his visit, before it came to an end. One day she suggested a change.

"Instead of coming for lunch tomorrow, would you like to come for dinner in the evening? It'll be even more atmospheric. I'm sure you'll love it."

He did not protest.

For once she did go to considerable trouble.

She managed to catch another couple of little emperor fish from the jetty. She was becoming expert at gutting them. She cooked some sweet potatoes and yams, plus prepared one of her now famous mixed salads with French vinaigrette sauce. She picked what she considered to be the best bottle of red wine that she could find, French even, with another one in reserve.

She tried to think of everything. She wanted this to be the dinner, the soirée, to remember - for him, Julien, but for her too. Who knew? It might be the only sweet memory which she had to hang on to during the coming months.

They seemed to be at their best, in that they seemed to enjoy it most, when talking about love and relationships, though they might be the two least qualified in the world to offer words of wisdom. Julien kicked them off tonight.

"Very often, two people fall in love with each other at the same time. They meet, they spend time together, they get to know each other and both find that they are falling in love with the other. I think that that was probably the case with my partner and me. We were both very young, perhaps too young. But I'm not going to say that that was why it didn't last. These things are never as simple as we sometimes want them to be, nor do they always follow a pattern."

"Don't I know! I think that if I had made a lifelong study, I would be no wiser today."

"Then you have the rather different situation where just one of the pair initially falls in love with the other. They either do or do not declare it. The timing can be crucial. But then interesting is the other person's reaction. Either they suspected before or not, but now they know that someone is in love with them. How should they respond? It's not always as simple as it seems."

To Alexandria it was simple.

"The person should look inside their heart, of course. They too might have been falling in love without quite noticing it. Now they have the chance to really examine their feelings. But it might turn out that, whilst they are extremely fond of the other person, it's not true love which they feel. The last thing that they should do is to force it, to try to generate a love which is not really there. It would not bode well for the long-term future."

"I don't disagree. But it's a tricky situation, isn't it? Especially if you have not been loved much or often in your life. If someone declares themselves to you, it can't be easily ignored. You have to ask yourself - 'Can I respond?' And you're bound to find yourself doing your damnedest to respond positively."

"I know. I've often been tempted. Do you know? On one occasion, with one particularly young man, one who I concluded afterwards was more dramatic than passionate, his declaration was so strong, so expressive and appeared so heartfelt, that I even entertained the thought - would his outstanding love suffice for us both? Fortunately I soon realised that it wouldn't, that the whole thing had little chance of working unless there was strong feeling on my part too. Once again I saved myself."

"I'm sure that you were right. If there are any cracks at all, they cannot be plastered over. It has to be mutual, a hundred percent, giving the whole heart, on both sides. No, one strong love will not do for two. It will break down in time."

"With me the boot has always been on the other foot. I always left it to the man to court me. I was always the pursued, never the pursuer. So I was often placed in the dilemma which you have just described. It would have been so easy to give my heart a little nudge, to try to tip it over the edge, to try to persuade it that it was in love or in time could fall that way. But I always caught myself in time, knowing that it would really be a type of self-deceit, unfair on the both of us."

"That I agree with."

"At the time or afterwards, I sometimes had cause to wonder if what they were offering was true love, I mean my idea of it, the real thing, the forever type. Put it like this - I often found out afterwards that most wasted no time in finding a replacement Alexandria, making me wonder about such matters as depth and longevity."

They both smiled. No-one was to be judged too heavily. In truth, no-one was to be judged at all. It was just human nature. We were all subject to it. This was not a blame game. We clutched at little straws of understanding but remained largely in the dark. Only the cynics who did not believe in it in the first place really escaped and then only to spend their lives in a bleaker landscape.

Chapter Twenty-Eight

Dinner was long over but neither showed any sign of wanting to terminate the evening. There was still plenty of wine left.

"It seems somewhat odd to me, a bit ironic, that we should obsess all our lives about something which often proves quite elusive."

Julien was getting quite used to her laying down these almost dramatic conversation-opening one-liners. He sat back, all ears, letting her expand.

"I mean to say - that this thorny problem of love has occupied mankind since the beginning of time and still does. It might seem a sweeping statement but without it there would be no great art. If you think about it - all the great masters, Titian, Michelangelo, all the great writers, Shakespeare, Cervantes, all the great musicians from Mozart to the Beatles, all the great actors and performers - what is it all about? At least 90%? But love! Without it, without its tormenting man's soul, there would be no Mona Lisa, no Romeo and Juliet, no Don Giovanni, no Jane Eyre, no Hey Jude, no Bohemian Rhapsody. It's like man and woman's obsession. Yet for most, does it always remain just a little out of reach? Is it that which keeps us going?"

Julien was listening intently, a smile playing about his lips as usual.

"I do believe that you are even more perceptive than me, Mademoiselle Alexandria."

"I know that you probably think me a little mad by now but I sometimes used to imagine the world as if it were different. When I was younger, I used to try to picture it with more honesty and sincerity in it, with less conflict, with less greed. It was just youthful indulgence. I even knew it at the time. Later on I tried to imagine a world without sex, I mean without the two sexes in it - either all-male or all-female. After all, it would be technically possible. Most plants and trees are of only one sex or are of no sex.

Even some creatures manage to reproduce without really mating. I mean, it would be possible. God could have created it that way if He had been minded to."

She paused for a moment, as if to allow Julien's imagination to catch up.

"But the thought of it sent a shiver down my spine. To me it seemed inconceivable. Or rather intolerable. Or rather completely without attraction. No, I had no man in my life, never had had. And yet to think of a world without men, well, it seemed completely pointless. It would take away my energy, my lust for life. In other words, despite my terrible track record, I needed that interest, still needed that incentive, that energy. Otherwise, everything would feel flat, pointless. I wouldn't want to paint, wouldn't want to grow anything, wouldn't want to sing, wouldn't want to make myself look beautiful. I know that I don't look beautiful but I used to do my best. When I think about it, it was really, in a convoluted sort of way, for love. I can't explain it any better."

"Mademoiselle Alexandria, you express yourself very well. I understand every word. And I cannot find it within myself to disagree with you, with a single word."

"It seems strange, again ironic, nor can I adequately explain it to myself, but I feel as if I know more about love than most others, even those who have spent most of their lives in a relationship or more than one. I don't know why but I just somehow feel more than think that my understanding is better, much deeper. It's as if they're too close to it, take it too much for granted, take it too much at face value. They have no time to stop and think, to really examine. I, on the other hand, have had tons of time, my whole lifetime, to ponder these matters. I've read no books on psychology, because no secrets of life, not even the secrets of the heart, are to be found there, just dry dead ends. The poets and painters get much closer, can teach us more. I even think that we can teach ourselves more, if we will only open up our minds and our hearts, get rid of all the fixed ideas, the straight-line thinking. I think that it was the Catalan architect Gaudí who pronounced that Nature had no straight lines and it was there that he found his inspiration. Well, I think much the same about thoughts and feelings, particularly about understanding. The open mind whizzes about, a bit like a kaleidoscope, a bit like electrons around a nucleus. They can go anywhere and come up with the most ridiculous ideas, even outrageous ones. Did you not yourself not say that this world of ours which we've created is crazy? That it needs setting upside-down? That's where my imagination goes. I let it because I trust it. It never comes back with anything less than interesting. More often than not it comes back with something true, very true. That's the fascination to me. And that's what I would write about if ever do commit my memoirs to writing."

Her eyes were sparkling. Julien looked at her and thought that he had never seen her look more alive, more animated, more excited. She was a woman of conviction, that was for sure. She would happily ignore all those experienced people with their wise old sayings. She would know different, would know truer. The answers were all inside us, if we cared to look, cared to delve deeply enough. Some children spoke more wisdom than their elders.

No, that did not describe her. She was no longer a child. But clearly she still had childish dreams, broken or otherwise. What was clear was that she was never going to let go of them. She would rather tend their grave, put flowers on it every Sunday. Yes, at the same time she would shed a tear, would experience a pang of regret. In the end the world, as it was, could not deliver. She was destined to be disappointed. At the same time she still felt that she had lived, had learnt, had grown. Again that was her conviction.

"Love is like a delicate little flower," she pronounced suddenly. "It needs looking after, needs very careful tending, otherwise it will wither and die."

"But that's only what you think, or think how it should be. You don't know for certain, not from experience. After all, you've never known love, not the real thing. I know that you rely on instinct but that's all that this is, isn't it? But it's yet to be confirmed by experience. The fact of the matter is that you've never been in love."

Once again he had his half-amused, ironic face on. Her expression was serious, subdued, almost timid. It was as if she did not know what to reply. Or did know but did not somehow dare. She contented herself with a one-line answer.

"I think what I think. I know what I know. I feel what I feel. And I know what I feel."

It was dark by now.

The garden was dimly lit by lights from the house and from other dim ones placed strategically here and there. It was atmospheric, even romantic. They chatted on in the same vein. The meal was over but it was still lovely to sip mouthfuls of the red nectar. And all overlooking a beautiful dark ocean.

She wanted to tell him. How much she wanted to tell him! How she wanted to pour out her whole heart to him! To tell him how much she loved him! From the bottom of her heart! How much she ached for him! How much she wanted to take him in her arms and press herself to him.

This time the boot truly was on the other foot. She wanted to declare herself. But somehow she could not bring herself to. And now she was going to hate herself afterwards, hold a resentment against herself for her lack of courage. Nevertheless, it had been a wonderful evening, one which she would never forget, ever.

Chapter Twenty-Nine

She did not sleep a wink.

They had spent such a pleasant evening. All the times which they spent together were pleasant but this latest one seemed to be better than all the rest, special somehow. They had talked so easily, at the same time keeping it light, even laughing and joking. If they had anything in common then it was that they both seemed to be able to laugh at themselves, more smile at themselves, at their follies, at the way they never fixed them but just went on to repeat them every time.

As usual it had been so convivial, eating together outside, watching the sun go down, seeing it dip below the waves on the far horizon. They had toasted it. They had toasted everything. Starting with a couple of tinnies of lager each, goodness knew how much wine they had got through between them. Okay, it was spread over the whole evening and accompanied by a meal but they must have got through a couple of bottles together. After all that, she should have slept like a top.

But she did not. In fact, it was as if she did not close her eyes all night. Not content with enjoying the aftermath of the evening, drifting into pleasant dreams, her mind seemed determined to question and probe, to almost turn in on itself, to go to dark places. Instead of pleasantly dwelling on what she had had, it seemed determined to concentrate solely on what she was about to lose.

After breakfast the following morning she strode across the island.

She found him sitting outside the beach hut, gazing at the ocean. They exchanged greetings. She sat down beside him.

"So you're leaving soon? Going on the next boat? It could be here at the weekend, tomorrow or the day after. Are you still decided on taking it?"

He did not reply immediately. He had not been expecting this sort of questioning and did not have any ready answers. He had to think for a moment.

"Well, I'll have stayed my month. That was what we agreed originally - wasn't it? - when I arrived. I mean - I don't want to outstay my welcome. You've been so kind, offering much better hospitality than I could have ever expected."

"It's been a pleasure. You know that."

"In any case, I've run out of money. I wouldn't have enough left to stay on for a further month. I need to get back to Grande Terre, to get back to work at the market there, to earn something. It's all right for you, loaded as you are. But I can't be on permanent holiday."

He was hoping to make her laugh but it did not work. Her expression stayed stony-faced. Her brain did not seem to be receptive to jokes this morning.

"The money isn't important. I could easily lower the rent to, say, half. You lend a hand about the place anyway, so effectively work for part of your keep. And as you well know, I don't do it for the money - put up guests, I mean. It's just nice having them around sometimes. It's just been so nice having you as a guest."

"No, but I wouldn't want to impose on you any longer, wouldn't want to keep on accepting your hospitality, all one-way, wouldn't want to feel that I was not paying my way, wouldn't want to feel that effectively I owed you money, wouldn't … … "

"Fuck the money!"

She immediately looked down and lowered her voice again.

"I'm sorry, Julien. I don't know what came over me just then. I'm just a bit on edge this morning, that's all. Your imminent departure seems to have unsettled me unduly, more than I thought it would, more that it should. But it's true nevertheless - that the money is unimportant and shouldn't be allowed to cloud the picture."

He did not reply immediately but kept his silence.

"Other than that consideration, is there any particular reason why you have to leave at the weekend? I mean, everything else being equal, the rest of your situation, is there any impelling reason for your needing to leave right now? Or would it be not so difficult to stay on a bit longer? Say, for another month?"

Once again he had to think, no prepared answers coming immediately to mind.

"To be honest, I hadn't thought about it. It's just that all along, almost since the day I arrived, my assumption has always been that my stay would be for just one month and then I would return to the main island and pick up things there again. But if you're asking me - Were I not to return this weekend, would I be letting anyone down? - then the answer is 'No'. Nevertheless, it still does feel as if I should leave, as I originally undertook."

It was her turn to pause. She wanted to find the right choice of words.

"I don't want you to leave, Julien, and I was hoping just now that you would say something similar - that you don't want to go either. But it's your decision and I respect that, totally. I just ask one more last thing of you. If you do go, will you promise me one thing? - that you'll come back one day?"

Tears were streaming down her face. She could not look at him. This had never happened to her before. Sure, she had cried, plenty of times, in private. But she had never done this before - almost begging a man to stay in her life when it was clear that destiny dictated that he left it.

Never had she experienced this depth of emotion before. It felt literally as if her heartstrings were being pulled inside her chest, stretched to near breaking point. She had hardly been able to complete her little speech and had not without her voice wavering. Now she could not go on, could not do anything, not even look at him. All that she could do was just sit there and quiver and let the tears flow.

Suddenly she leapt up.

Like a sprinter off the blocks, she propelled herself out of the chair and darted down the beach in the direction of the ocean. Even when she came to the water's edge she did not stop, her stride not faltering one iota. She just ran and ran, into the waves, carelessly, as if they were no barrier at all, as if she needed the water around her, to cover her, to wash away these stupid woman's tears.

Saltwater for saltwater. The two could mingle. And if by accident she should drown this day, then just at this moment she would not really mind. It might even be a beautiful end to it all. Maybe it was a good idea, just now, to shorten her future. After all, what did she have to live for? At this moment, floundering in the waves, instinctively trying to keep her head above the surface, she could not have answered.

She felt his arm around her midriff.

It felt so strong. It grabbed her and one thing was for sure - that it was not going to let go again. She felt herself being hauled back, hauled up, her whole neck and shoulders above the water now. She could breathe. She could shout. She could even still cry if she wished to.

For a moment they paused, as if the imminent danger were past, as if they both needed to get their breath back. All was quiet, just the sound of the waves. Neither spoke. What was there to say? She coughed up a little mouthful of water. She was fine. They both were.

Finally he released her. Instead, he gently turned her around to face the shore, looked at her and took her by the hand. She did not resist. Without any particular cue they started walking slowly back up the beach again.

It was as if in slow motion, their steps slow and short. To get back was taking a hundred times longer than it had taken her with her sprint. Finally they arrived back at the hut and resumed their respective places. No words were exchanged. It was as if there were none, not expressive enough.

She could not help it.

It was almost as if she were past caring, had nothing more to lose. So the chances were that he would leave as planned in a couple of days' time. So be it. Such was life. Nevertheless, before he went, she would allow herself one final indulgence. She turned to him, gently took his head in her hands and planted her lips against his left cheek.

And there they stayed. It must have been for a minute or two. He did not resist either, whatever was going through his mind. And she seemed so concentrated on the act, as if driven, as if at this very moment it were the only important thing in the world. No, it was not a kiss on the lips, just on the cheek. But she meant it every bit as much.

Chapter Thirty

Later on he called by for lunch as usual.

They were both quiet at first.

"I've been thinking," opened Julien. "I suppose that I could ask Émile to make my excuses at the market. I'll get him to tell them I'm in the middle of vital research."

Slowly the penny was dropping inside her head.

"Are you? Are you really staying?"

He smiled.

"It doesn't look as if I've got much choice!"

Now he was laughing. She was not. Her expression had never been so serious. In fact, she simply burst into tears again. He put his arm around her. After a few minutes she was calmer.

"This is so unlike me. Usually I'm not emotional like this. In fact, I'm sure that at one time I had a reputation as a bit of a cold fish. Certainly, some very handsome young men suffered because of me. Maybe I'm getting some of my own medicine now."

His arm squeezed her.

"I'm quite sure, Alexandria, that you are a very emotional lady. I know that you have a big heart. And I'm glad to see your tears. It shows that you care, care deeply. I think that's important. In fact, what is more important?"

The man on the tiller duly turned up on schedule, give or take a day or two.

Naturally, he brought over no new provisions for Julien, plus, bringing no new passengers, it meant that he had plenty of space for more than the usual supplies for Alexandria. They were a welcome sight. She duly paid him.

Julien joined them both on the jetty. In fact, he insisted on doing the bulk of the unloading. He knew where most things were stored by now. It was a welcome bit of work. He liked to feel useful too. When everything was duly stowed away, he returned to rejoin them.

The man on the tiller was looking around for Julien's bags but they were nowhere to be seen. Nor was the Frenchman making much of a move to board the little boat, wherever his belongings were, near or not so far away. It was a funny moment. It certainly made Julien smile.

"No, I'm not returning with you to Grande Terre, Émile. The fact of the matter is that the lady of the island won't let me. You must have lied to me, Émile. You told me that in the local language Motu Moemoea meant Islet of Dreams but it turns out to mean something closer to Alcatraz. Once a person sets foot on this island, there is no escape, no return, not without the say-so of the Empress Alexandria. So I have to disappoint you and commit you to a return journey on your own. See you in a couple of months or so. Have a word with them down at the market. Tell them that I've been unavoidably detained. Tell Matilda on the fish stall that I'll see her when I see her. She'll understand. She'll only laugh, just you see! But I will be over later in the year, when the real love of my life, daughter Mélodie, arrives in July. Make sure you come over for me before then. Otherwise I'll wind up having to send you a message in a bottle."

The man on the tiller was listening intently. He was too experienced to feel shocked or even surprised. He might just as likely merely shrug his shoulders. The number one lesson of life was always to expect the unexpected. People were queer anyway, unpredictable. You never really knew if you knew anyone, not really well. Anyone could surprise you and often did. He just did his job in life, tried to scrape a living, tried to build a good and happy home life. No-one could say that he did not succeed.

Meanwhile Alexandria was looking on in silence, not participating in the conversation, appearing somewhat undecided whether to be amused or irritated by Julien's habitual flippancy, mockingly portraying her as some dominant matriarch, when she could not really be at a further extreme.

Not for the first time, she decided to bite her lip and let it pass. The main thing was that Julien was not having a last-minute change of heart, was not going to ask the man on the tiller to hang on for another half an hour, while he made a mad dash back to the treehouse, to grab together his personal belongings, reappear and then make an equally mad dash for the boat, jumping in, not even giving her a kiss goodbye.

No, at least he was not going to do that. Because, if he did and if she now had to watch him sail away across the water, leaving her and her little island behind, then she really did think that it would break her little heart in two, never to me made whole again.

There was nothing to delay the man on the tiller any further. He could restart his engine and motor off. They both called after him.

"Bon voyage, Émile!"

Chapter Thirty-One

Very slowly, at just half pace, Alexandria and Julien wandered back up to the garden.

They both felt, she in particular, a little tired, emotionally tired. It had been an emotional time for her, over several days. But now everything seemed to be resolved, all parties happy. Now finally she could relax a little.

It seemed natural. She wanted to celebrate. It was before evening so she chose to go and fetch a couple of beers. It was so nice to be able to sit out in easy chairs in the garden round the table. For her the prospect seemed particularly agreeable. Now she had Julien for another month at least.

Not all to herself, of course. That would be asking too much. But she was happy with part of him, the contact which they had, the time which they spent together, the things which they shared, the company which they kept. Both of them seemed to be in a good mood now. They were just enjoying the day.

In fact, the first beer seemed to go down remarkably fast. No volunteers were needed to be called for to go and fetch another. It was such a lovely, smiley, Pacific afternoon.

Suddenly Alexandria was in tears again.

Clearly, it surprised Julien but did not seem to concern him unduly. Naturally he inquired as to the cause. She could not speak at first. Eventually, after another gulp of beer, she could.

"I've just had this picture running through my mind - of you and of Émile, sailing away in his little boat, looking back at me, smiling and waving. I try to smile and wave back but I can't, because I'm bent over double, retching my insides out, wondering if I'll ever be able to stand upright again."

She looked over at him. He got up and came over, knelt beside her. Her cheeks were still streaming with tears. He took her hand in his. She went on.

"I can only finally tell you this because now you can't run away, not for a little while, that is. I wanted to tell you the other night, during our lovely soirée together. I so wanted to tell you but didn't have the courage. Or rather, I didn't dare run the risk - of driving you away. Just a small part of me thought it might have the effect of making you change your mind and go back with Émile today, as originally planned. Although it was only a small risk, to me it was huge, not one which I could allow myself to take."

He squeezed her hand. She took a breath.

"I love you, Julien! I love you with all my heart. I know that we hardly know each other, have only known each other for a month. Normally I'd say that my heart would need six months, a year or more, to make its mind up, but this time it hasn't. I believe that halfway through the month it started - to fall. By the end of the third week it was certain, one hundred percent. Now it's cemented, with no going back. Whatever the future holds, I will always love you, Julien!"

She just sobbed away. It was as if it were all bad news. Or rather, it was as if she could not quite bring herself to believe that there could be a happy outcome. Okay, she would now have his company for a further few weeks. But eventually he would go, return to Grande Terre, there to greet delightful daughter Mélodie, in his own words the real love of his life. She, Alexandria, would soon be forgotten. Or just remembered as a pleasant enough interlude in a beautiful secluded spot out on the ocean, where he had done some more useful research and had an agreeable time into the bargain.

Now telling him, declaring herself, was probably going to make matters worse, if anything, perhaps put him off completely, maybe even render the rest of his stay awkward. She hoped not. He did not seem to be the sort to become awkward, embarrassed about things. It was just that she could not contain herself any longer. If she still had one honest bone left in her body, then she simply had to tell him, whatever the consequences. Now she had.

Still holding her hand, he got her to her feet and led her over to the three-seater canapé. They both sat down. He put an arm around her neck. She nestled into the dip of his shoulder. Their breathing, from the both of them, was heavy but slow. They sat in silence for several minutes. She seemed calmer now. Now it was his turn to speak.

"I'm glad that you did say what you said just now, that you've told me - that you love me, that you really truly love me. But I knew already. I've known for days, probably even before your spectacular plunge into the waves on the north shore, where I had to so dramatically rescue you."

A hint of humour was never far from his voice. It was as if he liked playing with recalling events and pointing up their humorous side.

"Throughout the whole month I could see you gradually, rather quite quickly, falling in love with me. It was unmistakable. You might not know it, Mademoiselle Alexandria, but you are the most transparent person whom I ever had the pleasure to meet. Sometimes you're even more transparent than a child, especially modern children. You have no guile, none of the waspish womanly wiles which often leave men dangling. You're like an open book, one I can read without difficulty."

It felt so good to be lying there, wrapped in his arms. How long she had dreamt of this moment. Perhaps all her life. Certainly for the whole of the past week. And now here it was happening.

And yet his words were not reassuring. Far from it. Everyone knew that those who laid their cards on the table never won the game. That - the role of victors - was reserved for those who played their cards close to their chest and revealed them the last.

Perhaps he was like that. At any rate he was telling her in no uncertain terms - that she lacked mystique. It was well known that most men loved a bit of mystique in a woman, almost demanded it. Yet she was completely lacking. What hope for her then?

Finally, in the second part of a life, past the menopause, she had succeeded in falling in love with the man of her dreams, only to guarantee at the same time that he would never reciprocate, would never be able to fall for her. So be it!

Yes, she would hate it, the day when he did eventually sail away. In the meantime she would simply try not to think about it. Just now she was not thinking about it. She was just lying in the arms of the man she loved, the only man she had ever loved.

Chapter Thirty-Two

"Will you stay with me tonight, Julien?"

That took even more courage. It was not that she had not thought about it from all the angles. She knew that she risked an even more painful and heartrending rejection then ever a man had received on a dance floor. She had not been unattractive in her day but the years always took their toll. Plus, no-one had to be a genius to know how most men viewed the idea of sleeping with an older woman.

What was their age gap in years? Neither had declared exactly but it could be all of eight or ten. Even apart from that, he might not even fancy her in the first place. No, once again she was playing a high risk game. Having played safe, the low risk game, all her life, now she seemed to have taken it into her head to become reckless, throwing caution, perhaps even modesty, to the winds.

Yet to her it did not feel like being flighty or flirty. She was just being herself, as usual. It was just that her feelings were different now. When that happened, convention dictated that they stayed hidden. But she was not following convention. The truth was that she never had.

Come nightfall she was exhausted, both physically and emotionally.

They were still outside. But she was falling asleep. He carried her inside, found her bedroom and laid her on her bed. She was wearing so little that there was no need to change into night attire. There was a sheet folded upon the pillow. He draped it over her, just covering her shoulders, planted a fatherly kiss on her forehead and left.

He called round early the following morning, his same old smiley self, but wondering how he would find her.

What was her same old self? The smiley one or the frowning

one? Which would he find today, especially after the events of the night before? He found her in remarkably good spirits, busying herself about, light on her feet, singing as she went. When she saw him, she stopped what she was doing.

"Time for morning tea break!"

A couple of minutes later she was bringing out a tray, very English. She poured, one cup with milk, one without. She sat back.

"I don't care what happens now. I sort of re-dreamt everything overnight, took stock of things during my sleeping hours. And this morning when I awoke, I realised - I've lived, finally I've lived! All my life I wanted to fall in love and now I have. All my life I wanted to tell him, my chosen loved one, and now I have. The rest is out of my hands. They say - better to have loved and lost than never to have loved at all. Well, I have now and, quite strangely, it has given me a wonderful warm feeling in my heart. Now I can go to my grave happy. But before then I will now relish every day and thank the universe for each one. This morning I am truly happy."

Julien was eyeing her up in his usual coy way, trying to read her face, her expression, her eyes. He did not miss much. Nothing much got past those qualities of discernment of his. He was taking it all in, computing it, now just waiting for the printout.

"I'm not going to say that I don't believe you, Alexandria, but I do have to tell you that I don't believe you fully."

She laughed. He was pleased to see it. They both laughed. This was much more like it, just like that time when she first surprised him on the north shore, sitting outside the beach hut. Then their shared laughter had broken through the ice, in fact had shattered it in an instant.

They had been like a couple of kids together, ready to roll in the grass. Now that spirit seemed back again. After all the heaviness of recent days, things were light again. The tea tasted delicious - to both of them. She poured two more cups. But she had to tell him something.

"Don't think that I'm asking for or expecting any commitment from you, Julien. You've already given me what I asked for - by simply agreeing to spending another month or two on the island with me. I won't ask you for anything more, I promise. I'm not asking for eternal love or anything like that. In fact, I'm not asking for love at all. Above all, don't think that you're getting into any sort of commitment, either long-term or even short-term. I expect nothing of you, other than to just carry on doing what you're doing, which, as you already know, is enhancing my life here. But what I do need you to know is that if one day you do decide to sleep with me - that is if you want to - I will not interpret it as any kind of commitment. I don't look to the future any more. Since I came to live here, I just try to live day-to-day. When next the boat comes, you will be free to go. On that I won't change my mind, I give you my word. You are as free as a bird. Well, perhaps not quite, because a bird could fly over the water back to the main island right now. You can't quite do that or even swim it. But as far as I'm concerned, you have your complete freedom. I would never try to tie you down."

As usual, he was just smiling back at her. More and more she was beginning to think that he did not believe a word she said, that he considered it all self-kidology, masking her real feelings underneath, which she dare not really voice for their being so old-fashioned and outdated.

He seemed to like to watch her going on like a novice orator, eventually tying herself in knots, saying things which were self-contradictory, inconsistent with her usual postures. He often refrained from commenting even, when she really wished that he would - at least say something, even if it were to catch her out, point out the inconsistencies, call her bluff. Instead, he downed the last of his tea.

"I need to go now. There's some work which I want to do up on the north shore. It won't be worth my coming back for lunch. Let's make it a late dinner instead. Just prepare something cold, light. I'll call round about dusk time. I know that it's a bit late but it won't have to matter for once. One late night won't hurt. It's just that I want to observe the birds, watch them swarming, just before sunset, to see if I can spot any patterns. But I won't be any later than I have to be."

It seemed a good plan to her too. She resumed her work in the garden till around noontime. She had a leisurely lunch. Just one beer seemed enough today. She resolved that she would wait for him that evening, not help herself to any drinks until he arrived. In fact, she had an idea, one which quite amused her.

Ever since coming out to Motu Moemoea, she had not had her hair cut.

There had been no good reason, plus also there were few decent hairdressers. Now it had grown to shoulder length, even a bit beyond. Just passing the bathroom mirror one day recently, she just got the fleeting thought that it made her look a little old. Nothing wrong with that. She was a little old. But she did not necessarily want to appear so, not before her time, and not just for Julien's benefit but for her own also.

So if he had a little plan for the day, then so did she. Since he would not be calling round before sunset, she would wait until the end of the afternoon heat, then she would bring out a large portable mirror which she had somewhere, place it strategically on a chair, kneel on the ground opposite with a pair of scissors and try to give herself the best haircut she could.

It might turn out a disaster. It might turn out okay. But it was not likely to put him off any more than he was now. And knowing the two of them together nowadays, it could at least be guaranteed to inject a little bit of jocularity into the proceedings. In other words, rather than admire her handiwork, he was much more likely to simply burst out laughing, she joining him.

After the haircut she would take a good long shower out in the garden, uninhibited, with all the birds watching but no human beings. Meanwhile, during the afternoon she would have chosen her most feminine and most youthful clothes.

Okay, she dressed for practical reasons these days, but she had brought over and kept a couple of especially pretty summer dresses, okay, a bit fussy, a bit frilly, a bit girly, a bit dated. They were not too long, the hem finishing just below the knee. But she had liked them once and, if she were honest, she still did now.

She was going to add one final little touch, a rather naughty one. She made her decision - she was going to wear no underclothes underneath, no bra or pants. She knew how revealing some summer dresses could be - the material light and thin, light in colour also. Plus, she had her all-over tan, with not a single streak or patch of white. But it would be dark by the time he arrived. He might not even notice. Or even care.

In a sense, she was doing all this more for herself than for him. How often had she dressed up sexy in her life? No-one need answer that question for her. Anyway, tonight, she was going to dress and feel sexy, if only for herself.

Chapter Thirty-Three

She executed the plan to perfection.

Okay, the haircut was perhaps not one hundred percent even all the way round but, looking at herself later in the bathroom mirror, she could honestly say that she had seen worse coming out of the hairdresser's.

She was happy with the choice of dress. Wearing it now, her body pristine-clean, almost glowing, she felt like a young woman again. It seemed to make her eyes sparkle. The sun was dropping lower in the sky outside. She was ready, as ready as she ever would be. In fact, she hoped that he would not be too long now.

He was not long.

In fact, if anything a little earlier than she expected, she saw him emerge through the garden gate. He was looking smarter too. He had also evidently showered and changed. He was wearing matching shirt and shorts, just off-white. As she watched him slowly approach, she thought him handsome, good enough to eat. If only he would let her take off the wrapping.

It was still a little before complete sunset. There was still plenty of light in the sky. In fact, it was a glorious time of day, perhaps the best, with everything and everywhere bathed in a yellowy-orange golden glow.

She stood to greet him but suddenly he stopped dead in his tracks.

He just stood stock-still for a moment, as if frozen. He just stared at her, his facial expression a mixture of astonishment, curiosity and amusement. It was as if he did not recognise her.

And yet it could not be someone else. The population of the island was too small for that. Meanwhile she was simply standing there, feet slightly apart, ready to hold out her hands in greeting and welcome. But he needed to get closer first.

Still he did not move or even say anything.

He seemed mesmerised. With her hair cut shorter, she had not been able to stop the part on top from sticking up a bit. Maybe it gave her a comical look, like out of a pantomime. She half expected him at any minute to burst into laughter. She would not mind. She probably deserved it and had even half engineered it. But he did not even do that. Instead, he still kept looking her up and down, from top to bottom, from bottom to top.

Okay, admittedly it was the first time that he had ever seen her in a dress before. Previously she had always been clad in shorts and T-shirt, at best a blouse. He had never even seen her in a skirt. But to see her now in a summer dress, in such a classic one, such that he did not think that they even made them like that any more, well it was a surprise, to say the least. Even out on a remote island, it was possible for one to surprise another.

His facial expression did not change much but finally, ever so slowly, he started inching his way forward again.

It seemed in slow motion. She started to do the same, just making little half-strides, barely one every ten seconds, just edging forward. As she did so, she could not help opening her arms out wide.

To him she seemed like a flower opening, a sunflower or something more subtle, like an orchid, no, more like a rose, one with that lovely tinge between white and yellow. Yes, it was as if he saw a white-yellow rose opening up and coming towards him. It was better than a Venus flytrap, that was for sure.

They both stopped a couple of metres apart. They were both looking each other up and down, but more than that, looking into each other's eyes. All four sparkled. Finally he reached out his arms too. Their hands touched. Then, still with no haste, still in slow motion, she entered his embrace, as he entered hers. It seemed like the first time.

They were each other's apéritif that evening.

In fact they had both lost their appetite - for both food and drink, that was. As the sun slowly sank below the surface of the ocean, they embraced and kissed, passionately for the first time.

Not long afterwards they peeled off each other's outer layering. How good it felt to be naked in the cool of the evening and at the approach of the oncoming darkness.

They devoured each other, leaving barely a body part untasted. They took their time. This could take all night. To her it was the first time in her life. To him it felt like the first time in his life. Never had the blood in their veins flowed so fast or so hot.

Finally he settled back in the middle of the three-piece canapé. She knelt astride him, putting her hands on his shoulders, dangling herself over his face. She lowered herself, again in slow motion. They both gasped. Finally they were one.

Chapter Thirty-Four

They made love again the following morning, on awakening, not outside in the garden this time but inside, on awakening, in her bed.

It was natural. They both wanted to. They did it with no less vigour, more if anything, energised by their long sleep. Maybe they took even longer, as if not wanting to leave any stone unturned, any nerve unstimulated, any desire unsatisfied, anything less than one hundred percent.

She could not help it.

She was walking on air. She really did feel that if she went down to the jetty, walked along its length, came to the end, but instead of stopping, kept going, then she would somehow not sink beneath the waves, but would soar up to join the birds. She was with them already anyway, flying around, singing sweet songs, feeling the air beneath her wings.

"Thank you, universe! Thank you, universe!"

She was only whispering it to herself but it was as if she could not stop. Yes, now, she could happily die without thinking that she had missed out on life. On the other hand, just now, death was the last thing on her mind, more the opposite. Having finally discovered life, she now just wanted to live it, to the full. Just now she could not get enough of life. It was literally intoxicating.

As a man, Julien would be expected to take it all in his stride.

He was a strong man, after all, not some silly romantic woman. Plus, this was not the first time for him. He had known love before, if some time before. In any case, if a man did lose his head over a woman, it behoved him not to show it. But he could not avoid it. Okay, there was no-one to see him making a fool of himself. The birds did not notice. He would not have minded if they did.

His way was to seek the security of the north shore, not so

much to seek refuge but to repair to familiar territory. He immediately stripped off and dived into the waves. He needed that, not the cold but the wet. Water was so sensuous. But also sensual. Just like love, it acted on the skin. Skin was living. He remembered having read somewhere -

'We think that we are our thoughts but we are our feelings. We think that we hear music but really we feel it. We think that we are our heads but we are our skin. We live not through the mind but through the body.'

He swam far out, in his inimitable lazy front crawl.

It was as if he lost sense - of both time and space. Before he knew where he was, he was far out enough to see the whole island, not exactly as a speck but as an entity, as if viewed from elsewhere. Just now he was elsewhere, as if in another world, looking back in.

He turned around. He wanted to go back to that other world. It was sweet now, sweeter than he had ever known it and that was saying something. He loved it for its own sake, especially the Nature. But now there was more, like another dimension, as if a new continent had been discovered and he had been appointed to lead the exploration.

Instead he would settle for exploring this little island which he was swimming back to. That would do for him. That would be big enough for him. He did not need a continent. He just needed a tiny part of one, an unknown little corner, almost neglected, almost wanted by no-one.

But it was not completely neglected. It was not completely unwanted. Someone was tending it. Someone was wanting it. And just now, all he wanted to do was tend and want and desire and love that person. That was his new mission in life, one which he was more than glad to accept, to grab with both hands. It gave him the sense of feeling at one with the world, as never before. It made him feel part of Nature herself. One thing was for sure - it was a good feeling, the best.

Chapter Thirty-Five

They still spent quite large parts of the day apart.

She was content to spend her mornings working. He continued to give her words of advice but he did not need to be ever-present. And now, more than ever, he seemed freed to concentrate on his own work. His research, more and more, was becoming a real project. More and more he was making it scientific, recording numbers, doing more precise sketches, recording all sorts of data.

There was a real chance now of putting flesh on the bones and of turning it into a genuine piece of first-class botanical and zoological research. Back on the main island one day, he should be able to write a paper and even get it published in one of the prominent scientific journals. What it meant was that he now had every incentive to treat this like a proper research programme rather than just a hobby. Nevertheless, he still found it fun.

He did not always return to house for lunch.

Some days they spent entirely apart, just as if he did go to work in the morning on the 8:23 and did not return till the evening on the 19:08. They often joked about it - that already they were like an old couple, overused to each other, set in their ways, the spark gone. How it made them laugh!

Nothing could be further from the truth. If anything, they were the opposite of all that - more like a young couple still on honeymoon. In an ironic way, spending time apart could not disguise the fact that they still could not get enough of each other.

More often than not, the evening meal met with the inevitably delay, would simply have to go by the by. There was not even time for an apéritif. If the word were supposed to signify something before, something to sharpen the appetite, it was coming to mean something nearer the opposite, something after, but still before the meal.

But before that there was some lovemaking to be done. They

would both be ready, keen and eager, both of them having been looking forward to it all day. And then, as he returned, it would be as if someone sounded a starting pistol. The floodgates opened. The race was under way.

But it was not a race, more a slow amble.

The initial embrace set them off. Each night it should be a welcome home, with a welcoming drink, a real liquid apéritif followed by a pleasant light meal, perfect. Instead, that initial embrace kindled a different type of appetite. Already they were salivating, but for something else, for each other. Once they got going, there was no stopping them, not until the race was run, until they both breasted the finishing line, almost all in.

Then, finally and only then, would thirst invade, and hunger. Only then would he go off to get the drinks, while she laid the table with the eats. It might be dark by then but that did not matter. There was no clock to watch. What could be better than supper by moonlight? Especially after making love? Beautiful love!

It was so doubly beautiful to do it outside.

It seemed freer somehow. They could shed each other's clothes, or at least half of them. Who cared? Often it was even more erotic to leave half of them on. Put it like this - this was the very opposite of any sort of bedroom routine. Or routine bedroom. This was still quintessentially fresh, new, young, almost innocent.

Yes, it still had that element of youthful innocence, that freshness. The desire came from deep within. Of course, there was the anticipation of pleasure, but more than that even was the desire to give pleasure to the other. As long as that took precedence, as long as that still led the way, they could keep that innocence and remain protected from the outside world. That was how it felt, being together and making love on Motu Moemoea.

The future could look after itself.

But one evening, 'afterwards', sipping wine and eating an unspectacular salad but with a fine French vinaigrette sauce, he reminded her of her erstwhile words.

"You said back then, when you were falling in love with me, but before it even looked likely that we would ever share a love, ever translate it into action, you said back then - that love was like a delicate little flower which needed much careful tending."

"And you reminded me that I didn't know what I was talking about, as I could not be speaking from experience, only from instinct, only from dreams."

They were both smiling in their gentle mocking way.

"Yes, I did, I admit it. But I didn't mean it. I liked to tease you back then, still do, but I knew even then that you were speaking from the heart, that you did in fact know what you are talking about. I could see it in your eyes, the way you looked at me. Life is full of ironies and that was perhaps one of the biggest. You were still a virgin, no longer a young one, but you knew more about love than I did, or indeed any man, the most experienced, or experienced woman. In fact, you had the confidence to say it - that they, the experienced ones, for some reason did the opposite, neglecting their love, just expecting it to go on living without special care. You'd seen it all around. You knew. But you also knew in your heart, felt it, that love was real and could last, if only it were treated like a tender little flower which needed watering and loving care each day. You had the wisdom which escaped others, probably the majority. And although I teased you and contradicted you a bit, I did know it, knew that you were right, that I had to hand it to you. Maybe that was when, that day, when I started to fall in love with you too."

She squeezed his arm and took another sip of wine. It tasted beautiful. Just now everything tasted beautiful.

Chapter Thirty-Six

They got into the habit of changing and dressing for dinner.

Okay, neither of them had any wardrobe as such. After all, he had only two shirts to his back and one pair of much repaired moccasins. She just had these couple of outdated summer dresses, plus a pleated skirt stuffed away somewhere, probably accompanied by a couple of classic blouses. But it was something. Just because they were living on a remote island with no-one else around did not mean that they did not have any standards to keep up.

It was a bit like when you went camping. Okay, during the day you were treading the trails, getting hot and sweaty, wearing your most practical gear - T-shirt and shorts, a scruffy pullover if it turned cold. But that did not mean that, arrived at your new location, camp all set up, tent, cooking equipment and everything installed, that you had to remain that way for the rest of the evening.

No, in fact it was nice not only to shower but also to put on a complete change of clothing, yes, if you had them with you, even if a few glad rags - a blouse or a smart shirt, a pair of longer shorts, a shawl against the cool of the evening. You could keep a civilised air about proceedings, making you feel good, clean, maybe even a little elegant, before getting back on the trails on the morrow.

Her haircut had done wonders.

It had taken years off her. It revealed her slim girlish neck. Without it, the summer dress would not have worked, would have looked incoherent somehow. As it was, the two had complemented each other perfectly.

But the coup de grace, even she had to admit, was her decision to wear no underclothes, no bra and pants. Whether she knew it or not at the time, she was presenting herself to him as one large Thanksgiving present. Not only that, but it was being presented within the most delectable wrapping, partially see-through, enough to make any man's mouth water. The all-over tan was indeed the coup de grâce, giving her that elusive mystique.

She might not quite have known it at the time, but that evening she had made her chances of landing her fish many times better than when she baited her lines at the end of her jetty, prepared, if necessary, to wait all afternoon. No, she knew what she was doing all right. She had dangled herself in front of him as prime bait at the hungry feeding hour and he was immediately taken - hook, line and sinker.

And now, if that it had worked, why change it now? People were not like fish, just landed once. That was the big mistake made, all over. You landed the catch and then you could relax, go back to your less attentive, more careless ways. The trouble was that many fish still did get away, even after they were landed.

So it paid to continue to take care, to pay attention to detail, to keep trying, above all to keep the attraction fresh. Hence her decision - to change and dress up every evening, that was, if leaving your underwear neatly folded away in its drawer, meant dressing up.

And the chances were that he, within his own constraints, would try to match her, would try to keep up. Just making an effort would please her well enough. That was all-important - keeping up the effort.

It meant that, most evenings, he could not wait for dinner to be over before he could get his hands on her. It also meant that their consumption, particularly of wine, went down, just a little.

How she loved being loved like this - he full of passion, she too.

Neither lacked for energy or desire. No two young sexual athletes would have left them in their wake. They would have found themselves being matched every inch of the way, being outlasted, just as long, if not longer.

She never failed to climax, sometimes more than once. When

he came, it was with a lion's roar, as if his whole being were erupting like a volcano, the most active in the world, the most deadly, spewing out his form of molten lava. It was dramatic. It was climactic. It was exhausting. It was beautiful.

How sweetly she slept afterwards!

She had always been a good sleeper, a natural one. She never needed any sleeping aids. Especially since coming to live out here, sleep seemed to come naturally with the darkening hours.

But now, each night, she was sleeping a sweet sleep. All her life she had waited for this, in fact, in quite a public grand gesture sort of way, had patently given up on it. She had even renamed her island, almost like putting up a public notice - 'No Entry!'

She had put up the shutters, hopefully for the final time. She was going to live out the rest of her days in this delightfully simple way, all alone, with just the birds and animals for company, which meant with no human beings, certainly no male ones.

But how all that had been so dramatically turned around in the most unexpected way! Even now, she could scarce believe it. Maybe she should pinch herself, to make sure that it was not all just a silly dream, like the ones which she used to have, when she was seven, when she was seventeen.

Now she was back to having those dreams on a regular basis. The difference now was that it meant that they were also accompanied by an even more delightful reality. Dreams were beautiful. Living was better. Making love, she was discovering, was the best living of all.

It was different for Julien too.

In a way it took away some of his independence, his supposed self-sufficiency. Before, he could take her or leave her. How close in truth had he come to taking that boat back? What in truth had decided him in the end to stay? Did his interest in her only account for half of it?

In other words, did the chance to spend a couple more months doing more precious research account for the other half? And when she had first effectively offered herself to him, he had not taken advantage but had kept his powder dry.

Now the boot was truly on the other foot. Now he relished her, wanted her, desired her, every night. Yes, he, Mr Independence, the amused observer, no longer was, quite, all those things. No, now he needed her. Very soon, very suddenly, Alexandria had become the centre of his universe. He could not stay away.

He did not want to stay away. Nor could he keep his hands off her. Who was the real love of his life now? If hitherto he had always enjoyed pointing to delightful daughter Mélodie, just now he might have to reflect a while before answering.

In fact, for the first time in his life, he found himself wanting to tell the one about the other, not just wanting, almost desperate. Yet the means of communication simply was not there.

Just as she, daughter Mélodie, could not contact him, not even in an emergency, only her mother, so he now could not send her his very overdue good news. It would have to wait until the European summer, when he would see her again in person. It was hard not to be able to tell her before but there was no alternative. He would have to be patient.

Chapter Thirty-Seven

Some afternoons they spent, the two of them, swimming off the north shore.

In truth it had good memories for them, even the beach hut. It sometimes still made them laugh, just to see it, in the shade of the palms, remembering the rather dramatic - or was it comical? - scenes acted out between them there.

The swimming was good there, the waves big and juicy, something of a challenge, although he never quite had to rescue her again. Back at the beach hut, seated outside, sharing a drink, it seemed appropriate to reflect.

"It's funny - how things work out sometimes, isn't it?"

Once again, it was a thought which either of them might have voiced. Julien smiled before replying.

"I think, Mademoiselle Alexandria, that you have good reason to feel vindicated."

"But it wasn't my doing! I didn't bring you here! In fact, I nearly sent you packing, even before you'd set one foot on my jetty. So I can't claim any of the credit!"

"I meant - more beforehand, the way that you stuck to your beliefs, never gave in, even when the chorus around you must have been deafening. You still stuck to your guns, didn't give in, even went so far as to distance yourself from it all, even at the expense of facing a lonely future. I don't know many people who would have done that, including myself. So you do deserve the credit really, even if you don't feel it."

"There have been lonely times, I can't deny it. And it's funny again. You sort of get used to it - the loneliness - but in the end you never do, not completely. You accept it. Or rather, I accepted it, as just part of life, as part of the hand which was dealt me. But I never wanted it, never really enjoyed it. There just seemed no alternative."

"But crucially, you never closed your heart. You'd be

surprised how many do, especially as they age. I've met loads of women, say more or less around your age, who, having suffered hurt in the past, have turned their heart off, have closed it up or have surrounded it with a shield. Their priority becomes simply not to be hurt again. But what they don't all realise is that if you put a shield around your heart, not only do you keep out the potential pain but you also keep out the potential love too. They can't have it both ways, even if they seem to want to."

"Maybe it's because they've suffered more than me - the pain of a breakup, maybe even of betrayal."

"I think you suffered just as much as them, Alexandria. It's all relative. They at least had the joy of love, at first at least, even if it was not to last forever. And everyone suffers, sooner or later. One could argue even that you had a lifetime of it, always living on the outside, never being admitted to the inner sanctum. That can't have been easy. That's why I say that you were strong to resist the temptation - to throw in your hand of cards and get a new one from the dealer, one marked 'compromise'. But you never did."

"It wasn't that difficult. In truth, the temptation was never that strong. It's not that the inner voice was loud, because it never is. But it was firm in its quietness, confident. Put it like this - it never stopped saying to me - 'Trust me! I'll never let you down!' "

She gave a wry smile before continuing.

"But I must admit that I once came close - I mean, to distrusting it, to abandoning it, to stopping listening. Ironically, it was in the run-up to my big decision - to come and live out here. By this time I'd done the first trip to New Caledonia, had visited the islet, had agreed in principle to buy it, but having paid nothing and signed nothing, I still had a way to back out. I went back home but told no-one, probably for fear of being laughed at, of being thought mad. But then I thought to myself much the same - that it was a ridiculous project, laughable, that there was indeed a strong possibility that I was becoming insane, was losing my marbles, had almost become a fanatic, clinging on to some outdated principles which went out, not at the end of the twentieth century but more likely at the end of the nineteenth, when Emile Zola died and Marcel Proust was born, when Thomas Hardy stopped writing and D. H. Lawrence started, when Verdi faded and Puccini rose, when Sigmund Freud appeared and spawned fellow Austro-German writers like Frank Wedekind and Arthur Schnitzler. Put it like this - the moral climate had begun to change a whole century before. And there was me - still trying to fly the flag like some ridiculous member of the Flat Earth Society. I mean to say - even I had cause to question the validity of the whole thing, to question myself."

"That's never a bad idea, especially if the end result is to remove all doubt."

"I had never much liked, whenever and wherever I had seen it, excessive religious zeal. I thought it unbalanced and unbalancing. I had always advocated moderating it, such that it could coexist in the real world. And yet here was I - on the verge of doing a passable imitation of similar zeal, albeit without the religion. Did that mean, even, that I had even less excuse? They at least were doing it for God. I was only really doing it for myself, for some misguided idea of integrity. Put it like this - as I thought on, the cracks started to appear and yes, the self-doubts were creeping in. Was I about to make the most monumental mistake, one which would be difficult to reverse? I spent a few sleepless nights, I can tell you."

"At least you could not be accused of rushing it, of being impulsive. At least you gave yourself time - to reflect."

"And it's funny - the way my thinking turned, the way that the thought process went. Here I was, about to sell up and leave the country of my birth in order to go off and live in isolation on precisely the other side of the world. And my mind was telling me, this infernal little voice inside - that there was no alternative. In other words staying, whether it was continuing in my job or retiring early, simply wasn't an option. Or rather, staying around, more or less continuing as before, could only be a formula for further isolation, for more misery, even worse because every day, looking around at other people, I would be reminded of it. No, as my mind worked throughout those sleepless nights, it could only come to one conclusion - that it had to be the clean break. Anything less would have led to a kind of purgatory, not to be endured. It was better to do the full leap than half. That way, at least, there would be no coming back. That's what I needed - that finality. And that's what in the end decided me."

Julien had no more words to say. Or maybe the ones which came to mind seemed to him trite, unworthy of rounding off her heartfelt little speech.

The trouble was that, after the afternoon swims on the north shore, invariably followed by a drink and conversation, they invariably wound up making love, either inside the beach hut or outside.

Having listened to her, having watched her express herself so clearly, so sincerely, so honestly, invariably Julien found that he could not keep his hands to himself. He wanted her, there and then. He desired her. He hungered for her. He could not hold back.

She too would now be in a heightened state, feeling emotional, therefore responsive. One move from him and she felt the same desire surge up within. It was like a little powder keg. All it needed was a spark. Invariably there were two sparks. The powder keg never stood a chance. Each time it was blown to smithereens!

Chapter Thirty-Eight

The secret of life lay in having low expectations.

Like everything else, that could be turned on its head to explain the other side of the coin.

Why, in prosperous societies, in the lands of plenty, was there such widespread depression? In no way did it make any sense. Surely, depression should surround the poor family, half surviving in the Third World. Yet the opposite was true. There it was impossible to keep smiles off faces. Meanwhile, the mournful face was reserved for the so-called rich nations.

The explanation lay in expectations, high ones, probably too high. It was the way that the children were brought up. Add to that, omnipresent visual advertising, TV series and the rest of popular culture, modern electronic technology and virtual living, and you arrived at an almost toxic mix, enough to derail and even disturb the best adjusted people of all ages. The result? A depressive state of mind. The answer? Medication, probably long-term.

Sometimes in life, rarely perhaps, it was possible to change those expectations.

One needed to find a way effectively to lower them. Somewhat coincidentally and completely separately, both Alexandria and Julien, almost certainly unintentionally and unconsciously, had managed to do precisely that. Their total expectations had finished up not just low but non-existent.

They had none, none other than the simple hope that the sun would rise the following day. Suddenly - it was indeed sudden - all that changed. Or rather, something happened to both of them which was beyond their wildest dreams. In almost an instant they went from zero to one hundred percent. Now that was how to find true happiness.

There was another secret - if you received joy from life,

appreciate it!

It was all part of the same mentality. Maybe it could best be described using another word - always stay humble!

Neither of them had realised, of course, during the run-up, leading their separate lives. And to some extent it was the harsh lesson of a disappointing life which taught them, such that they had both and separately, unlike most, come to know humility. It was a precious ally. Often shunned, often mistrusted, but in truth the most reliable ally of all - manage to keep it and you kept at bay all those western ills, possibly for ever.

It meant that they were not just happy, they were deliriously happy.

What had she been thinking? Only a relatively short while before? - 'I'll live out the rest of my days here, just me, the sand and the sea. I'll just live here, alone with my broken dreams.' Now she could not say that any more. Now she had to turn around and go to the other extreme and say something like - 'Now I'll spend every day with the man I love.'

No, even now, it paid not to look too far ahead. That was all part of the humility. It still paid to take nothing for granted. In fact, it still paid to keep, if she could, those expectations low. That way, every day was a bonus. That way, every moment spent with Julien was a bonus. That way, especially, every time they made love together was a bonus.

Life with bonuses. Better than life with shortfalls. That was the key. It was like tipping the world upside-down. But looking around, the world needed tipping upside-down. Only then did it look the right way up. Only then did it feel the right way up.

For Julien it was similar. He too seemed to have become resigned never to find another love. He could try as much as he wanted to do a kind of love transference, to promote his daughter, to try to centre a kind of love life around her. But that could never succeed, not wholly. Old unsatisfied needs would surface eventually, not exactly to haunt him but certainly to disturb him, to reduce his enjoyment of life.

Yes, they were both doing right - to return to Nature, to live as closely to her, in hand with her, as much as possible. But even Nature could not satisfy the whole man. There would still be left a yearning, unsatisfied.

But now, completely unexpectedly, that yearning was fulfilled. He too had gone from one extreme to another. If he too had the wisdom from somewhere, to know that he was fortunate, then he should remind himself every day. Maybe just now he was the happiest man in the world.

Chapter Thirty-Nine

"It's funny but I never felt like a misfit or anything."

It was after lunch, with neither of them in any hurry to get on with anything specific. They often talked like this. One or the other often had something on their mind, wanting to express it. Julien looked at her, as always waiting for her to expand.

"I could be in any place - in the countryside where I grew up, in our house or garden, practising piano or painting a woodland, walking in the mountains, swimming in the sea, learning French or mathematics at school, even certain nights at the theatre or in the concert hall. The list could go on - but I felt absolutely at one with the world. Just for a moment, an hour or a few, everything seemed perfect. I think that I felt a closer harmony - both with the outside world and within myself - than anyone else I knew. No, it was not that I was not meant for this world, that I was a reject, an outsider. I was the opposite - an arch-insider, right at its core. It was almost as if the world had been designed for me in all its glory - Nature, music, beauty everywhere. Put it like this - it really satisfied my soul."

Julien was listening to her every word, knowing how carefully they were being chosen, what weight each had. She continued.

"I was just completely unprepared for one thing - duplicity. Or in other words, I was in tune with everything - all the environment, even all the animals, without exception, or rather, with just one exception - the so-called highest, homo-sapiens. To me it was that one, that one alone, who spoiled the party."

"You've probably just hit the nail on the head."

That seemed to prompt her.

"I mean to say - it's difficult, looking around, to come to any conclusion other than that mankind has made a huge mess of things. Just look around! - Little wars everywhere, so much conflict, so much violence. The Americans even dropped a couple of atomic bombs. It was almost as if they couldn't wait to try them out, particularly the second."

She paused again, as if gathering her thoughts.

"Wherever man has gone, he hasn't exactly brought beauty or harmony, nor has he been motivated by noble ideals. Greed seems to be the driving force. That's the only reason why we are losing the rainforests. It's not the locals who are doing it. It's not the native people who benefit, just big business. In fact the locals suffer, seeing their traditional environment destroyed before their very eyes."

A tear ran down her cheek.

"It's all that that I couldn't fit in with. But it's not me, the misfit. It's man. I and a few others could live in perfect harmony with this world and all its creatures. It's just man, I mean the majority of mankind, who can't, who won't, who will destroy anything and everything, all in the name of materialism, nothing more, nothing less."

The tears did not seem to be for herself, more for the planet, sort of mourning its passing, the loss of its bloom.

"So I wasn't born out of my time really. I would have still struggled, had I been born earlier or later. Yes, our age does seem the maddest but the insanity began long before, a couple of hundred years ago at least, when man decided to turn his back on Nature and put all his faith in science. Sure, he kept on going to church but really it was back then that he stopped believing in God and began to believe in himself, as a kind of new God, in his own ability - to know everything, to be the master of everything. He lost his humility, never to be regained again. That was the real hubris. That is what is really bringing down fire from heaven now, why we are being visited by plagues and worse. It's the hubris of man. He is heading for the cliff edge, I'm convinced of it. The irony is - that he can't see it, because he no longer trusts his senses, his instincts. He is putting all his faith in machines now and they will, I believe, ultimately destroy him, become his master, he the slave. It is ironic, isn't it? It would be almost funny, if it weren't so tragic. I still believe that it's avoidable. But I don't think that it will be avoided. No, there's too much momentum now, a real head of steam. The cliff edge looks like the promised land, machines doing all the work. Only then will man be satisfied. But also only then will he lose the will to live."

The tears had stopped flowing but she still looked sad. Julien had never seen her like this before, heard her speak like this, so profoundly. It was all so heartfelt, almost personal, as if she were Earth's advocate, the defender. But alone she was powerless. The forces arrayed against her were too numerous, too strong. It was a losing battle. It was one which she seemed resigned to losing.

He took her by the hand and squeezed it. She gave a wry smile.

"At least I've got you, Julien. At least I've got Motu Moemoea. Both give me the will to live, the will to protect and nurture this forgotten little corner of a much greater whole. This is my destiny now. This is where I fit in. And believe me! - Although I might not look it tonight, I'm so happy, so happy inside. I know that it will sound strange, a bit cockeyed, the reverse of the conventional way of saying. We might have lost the war. But we can still win the battle."

He squeezed her hand again, as if not just for encouragement but in admiration. Who was the little amateur home-spun philosopher now? More importantly, who had the biggest heart?

Chapter Forty

"I wanted to ask you something, Alexandria."

It sounded serious but as usual his expression was light.

"When I go back to Grande Terre in June or July, in order to welcome Mélodie, if she should show some interest in wanting to visit Motu Meomeoa, to spend a bit of time here, would you be able to accommodate her? Would she be welcome here?"

It was her turn to laugh. She could not find it in herself to be as annoyed as she perhaps should be.

"You know that you don't have to ask me - something like that, Julien. Any member of your family would be most welcome here, as would be any dear friend of yours. I would be only too delighted to receive a visit from Mélodie. In fact, I'm dying to meet her. And if a visit from her would avoid my having to travel over to the main island then all the better. From what you've told me about her, I think she'll love it here just as much as we two do."

Later on he mentioned it again.

"Come over with me, Alexandria! We'll both go to the airport and bring Mélodie straight back here. You won't even have to spend the night there on Grande Terre."

"No, Julien. Thank you so much for asking but it's not my place to be there. It's yours and yours alone. I wouldn't want to impinge on that special moment. The two of you won't have seen each other for nearly a year, so it will be special, very. It's a moment for father and daughter reunited, that so special bond, like that between mother and son. It's yours to enjoy to the full, for the both of you. Even spend a few days together, if you like! Catch up with the market! See Matilda! Make her laugh! You could even do a little touring of the main island, taking a little holiday, just the two of you. I'll be fine here, happy to do a few preparations, but above all looking forward to hearing the chug-chug of Émile's little boat, bearing the two of you across the waves, not just you two but bringing plenty of lovely provisions too, especially the liquid ones."

It was probably at the beginning of June.

Things were going well but Julien's thoughts, inevitably, were turning increasingly towards his next trip, probably before the end of the month, when he would be heading back over the water with the man on the tiller, the objective this time meeting Mélodie off her aeroplane.

It might feel strange again, to be back on the main island again, back within the bosom of civilisation. How would he feel after such a long break away? Ambivalent? That was the thought with which he seemed to be wrestling just now, trying to anticipate how he would feel.

The suggestion was to do a bit of touring together, the two of them, just a few days. But should he also take advantage? - to spend another half-week knocking his research project into shape? It would be pointless to leave it permanently in rough draft form. Often it was best to strike while the iron was hot.

The trouble was - if he did spend a whole week or more on Grande Terre, would the old ties start to bind him again, wanting to hold him back? It was still human nature always to take the easy option. Often it took guts, courage, to take the more difficult one. Somehow, just now, he did not know how much he could trust himself.

It was later in the day, when music was, as usual, wafting from inside out into the garden.

He happened to catch eye of the laptop. That was all that it was used for now - playing music. And yet, if he thought about it now, it could be used in its other functions, those that normal people used it for, in particular the preparation of documents, sometimes quite sophisticated ones. In a nutshell, with any luck he should be able to make great progress on his project here on the little island, maybe even finish it.

He was almost kicking himself. Why had he not thought of that before? At the same time a cloud seemed to lift from his brow. Suddenly he could see clearly again. Suddenly he knew where his future lay and it was not back on Grande Terre or indeed in any part of that outer world.

Somewhat to Alexandria's surprise and perhaps to his own surprise too, Julien followed her proposal to take a short holiday with Mélodie.

It was a long and tearful reunion at the airport. Father and daughter celebrated it with a meal out at the restaurant opposite the market, the cheapest in town, with its rough wooden tables and chairs, but also the best, serving the finest of fish lunches and suppers, the seafood supplied, needless to say, by Matilda's stall, accompanied by rich local wine.

The following day they did go to the market, not to work, more to rib Matilda on the fish stall. She was delighted to see them too. If she could, she would have taken a two-hour lunch break to join them across the road.

It was Mélodie who had to hire the car. Julien had never learned to drive. She had to pay for it too. He had no money either. Fortunately she was no impoverished student. No, she did not work yet, in fact had only, literally within the last week, finished her studies.

Was it better to have a close loving mother or a distant guilt-stricken one? Mélodie had no choice in the matter but if she had had to forego the advantages of the first, then she might just as well make the most of the advantages of the second.

The result was that she had the biggest bank balance of her year. It also meant that she could visit her father without delay, halfway across the world. It also meant that she did not have the worry of the vast majority of her fellow graduates - finding work, almost any work, and immediately.

Chapter Forty-One

They spent a wonderful three days, touring the main island.

They visited places which they had never even heard of before, never mind visited. With the car they could get to the most remote spots, where few other Europeans ventured. Okay, it meant that much of the overnight accommodation was cheap and cheerful, basic, to say the least. But that was all part of the adventure. They both relished it. They even joked about it.

"So is this what it's like on Motu Meomeoa, Papa? This remote desert island you're planning to take me to? Shall we say? - without many home comforts?"

He nodded.

"Much the same! In my treehouse there is no glass in the windows. The beach hut on the north shore, like most of the those little outbuildings, is roofed with grass. There is just one shower on the island, unheated of course, but with no walls around to prevent prying looks. So it's not for the faint of heart."

None of what he said was a lie. But he just remembered. Thus far he had not spoken to Mélodie about Alexandria. Unlike normal families, they did not use electronic communication to keep in touch while apart. He had not been able to pre-warn her of anything which had happened in recent months.

It was like an unforgivable oversight but everything else just seemed to have crowded it out. What a gaffe! How could he explain? But now, out here in this remote place on Grande Terre, now finally there was the time and opportunity. He took a deep breath.

He just told it how it was - from his hearing about the island from Émile, his chilly reception on arrival at the jetty from the irritated owner, about the ice melting, about them talking more, quite regularly and about personal experiences, becoming in the end quite close, and not just friends, certainly more for her, she declaring herself, he still unsure, until one magical evening, when he quite simply fell head over heels for her and had to have her, there and then, outside in the twilight.

"Why, that's wonderful, Papa!"

She rushed over to embrace him warmly, flinging her arms around his neck and bring him close, planting a big wet kiss on his cheek. She resumed her seat. She also resumed her speech.

"Why, that's the best news I've heard in years. You've been alone for so long, far too long. I almost thought that you had turned away - from the chances of love, I mean - immersing yourself instead in your other passion, for plants, for Nature. But we all need someone, Papa, even you. And now you've found her. But an older irritable Englishwoman? Surely you could have chosen better!"

She was laughing. So was he. They held hands for a moment. Yes, father and daughter reunited.

Meanwhile back on Motu Moemoea, Alexandria was not completely idle either.

She worked the mornings as usual. She wanted to have a good and varied supply of fruits and vegetables to welcome her imminently arriving guests. But after the heat of the afternoon it was time to devote time to herself again, to try to make herself as presentable as possible.

It was not so much that she wanted to impress Mélodie. There was not much chance of that. But she could avoid the other extreme, letting herself down, appearing unkempt, uncared for and just plain frumpy. She had achieved a little transformation once, only a few months before, which had worked in her favour. Time for a little refit, for another mini-transformation.

Out came the heavy portable mirror again. Out came the scissors. She took no greater care. She knew that the result would be a little uneven here and there. So be it! It was all part of the effect. She wanted to keep a little bit of wildness, almost create some.

In fact, this time she would be even just a little bit more daring, make it a fraction shorter, so that the hair did stick up on top, like a shock. That way it revealed her slim girlish neck even more, gave her, she hoped, that fresh clean look, with her round face, almost boyish.

Just like the last time, it might not come off. More than that, it might just make her look a little ridiculous - someone old trying to look someone young. She took the risk. Once again, at worst it would just cause laughter. That would not represent too bad a type of failure.

She also had to choose her attire, for when the boat arrived, to receive the little French family. Not the summer dress this time. It would be too early in the day. No, this time she would opt for something between that and her working clothes - blouse and skirt.

She inspected them. Yes, clean and fragrant, even a little simple and smart, even if she did say so herself. She laid them out for the morrow. But who knew? It might be the morrow of the morrow when they finally turned up. Or even the day after. Such was the way of life around here. But she was glad of it. Above all, she just hoped in her heart of hearts that Julien and his daughter Mélodie were safe somewhere and were having a wonderful time.

They were.

In fact, they did prolong their tour by one extra day. There just seemed to be no sense not to, if it meant that they could reach a further fascinating little corner, another promontory overlooking the ocean, another little village off the beaten track, so unused to visitors that there was no proper restaurant. But 'Table d'hôte' could be delightful and was, plus a chance to get to know the locals a bit.

Julien was delighted. Mélodie was enchanted. All in all, they could not have spent a better holiday together. But now it was time to head back to the capital, to return the hire-car, to seek out Émile and travel across that long stretch of water. Time to go home.

Could he call it that? Was it really home to him yet? It was not a thought that he had to consider. The truth was probably nearer that, just now and for the past few years, he did not really have a home, not unless he included the country of his birth, where he had lived in France. Where was home? Where you came from? Where you were going? At any rate, just now they were heading for Motu Moemoea, the home of an older irritable Englishwoman.

Chapter Forty-Two

Alexandria thought that she heard it.

She stopped to listen. If she were right, if it were the chug-chug of the boat which she heard, the timing was quite bad. No, she was not caked from head to toe in thick black mud. But she was in her sweaty working togs.

How could she not be? She could hardly wait for them day after day in what she termed her 'reception clothes', in this case her blouse and skirt. She could not work in those. Nor could she stay idle all day. But she had devised a little plan, what she liked to think of as her little military operation. Now, distinctly hearing that chug-chug far out on the water, it was time to throw it into action.

There, on the spot, in the garden, she stripped naked and bundled all her clothes, wrapped up into a ball, which she stowed in the out-building which housed the tall fridge with the beer.

She dived under the shower. It felt gorgeous. There was soap and shampoo to hand but no walls to hide her. But anyone on the incoming boat would need binoculars and if they were bringing those, it was probably more to look at the birdlife then to do a peeping Tom on her while she was showering. She even took her time.

The towel was already there, laid out close by. In particular, she was anxious to dry her hair well, although, so short now, after a good rub, it would dry itself almost completely in just a matter of minutes. She moved inside without rushing, knowing that there was still in truth plenty of time. In the mirror she used her fingers as a comb to calm her wild hair a little.

Once again, everything was laid out, pre-planned. She even remembered underclothes this time, a matching white pair of bra and pants, brief, even a bit sexy, lovely and clean and fresh-smelling. They should not show too much underneath the rest of what she would be wearing, predictably, the white blouse and short pleated beige skirt, which finished just above the knee.

The final touch - a lovely light pair of matching beige moccasins, the best she had. When finally she was ready, she appeared as if she might just be leaving to take part in a game of lawn tennis.

But now the chug-chug of the approaching boat was getting even louder. It was time to go and meet her guests, to go to be the welcoming party, to go to face the music. One last look in the mirror, one last tweak of her hair, a little smile to herself and she was ready. She had done little rushing. But it was time that she slowed back down to slow motion pace.

She waved from the jetty, as the faces on the boat became recognisable.

All were smiling, even the face of the man on the tiller. He had grown quite fond of her now too. He looked forward to these irregular visits. He glided up to the jetty in that inimitable gentle manner of his, barely touching. The boat was soon moored up.

She first helped Mélodie off, although she did not really need it. Then she helped Julien off, although he did not really need it. She embraced him, long and lovingly. Then she turned to Mélodie.

"Mélodie, my dear, I can't tell you what a pleasure it is to meet you."

They too embraced, perhaps surprisingly long and lovingly, considering that they were meeting for the first time. It was time for the clichés, though they were sincerely meant.

"I've heard so much about you, Mélodie."

"And I about you, Alexandria."

She might have added - 'all about the old irritable Englishwoman'. But the woman who had just embraced her so warmly looked anything but. Why had her father deceived her so? Instead, it was left to Alexandria to expand her welcome.

"I really hope that you have the most wonderful time here on my humble little island, Mélodie."

Julien, naturally, was just looking on, totally amused. Maybe he had painted Alexandria - shall we say? - more according to her disadvantages, out of his little sense of mischief. Now, to see her looking at her best again after the second mini-transformation, to see the look of confusion but contentment on the face of daughter Mélodie - to him it was such an amusing and happy outcome.

He helped the man on the tiller unload the provisions.

The two ladies walked towards the garden, to the semicircular three-piece suite surrounding the low-slung table. Alexandria saw to it that Mélodie was comfortable. She would not make her wait long before serving them all a drink. But she had to go to pay the man on the tiller.

"Thank you so much once again, Émile. You really are a treasure. I don't know what I would do without you. Here's your money. But please let me give you a little extra this month, just by way of a thank-you for everything you've done for me ever since I arrived here, a few years ago now."

She handed him another banknote. He just stared at it for a moment, as if it were a strange unrecognisable piece of paper which no-one could make head nor tail of. It was almost as if he had never seen one before, never such a large banknote, not one for 10,000 francs CFP. Almost reluctantly, eventually he reached out his hand and took it.

"Thank you, Mademoiselle Alexandria. Now I will be able to treat my wife and children. I will be able to buy them things which they cannot normally have. We will live well for a month, all thanks to you, Mademoiselle."

"You deserve it, Émile, every centime! Go and be happy with your family! See you again next time, in a couple of months or so!"

He left.

Meanwhile Julien was carrying a full tray of drinks down to the corner of the garden where sat the waiting Mélodie.

Soon all three of them were comfortably seated, each with a glass in hand, Alexandria and Julien on the three-seater canapé, Mélodie in one of the accompanying armchairs.

Already on day one, Alexandria and Mélodie showed every sign of getting on famously.

It was curious how these connections could soon be made, with just with a few gestures, a few looks, a few words. It sounded absurd but already their friendship seemed to be destined to become less an inter-generation relationship, more one of sisterly complicity and feeling.

Already they were chatting about this and that, joking about similar things which they had found back in the outer world, probably also sharing a joke at the expense of the father of the one and the lover of the other, poor Julien.

But needless to say, it was all done in a generous spirit. They were glad finally to meet each other and to have that opportunity in such circumstances, in such a relaxed location. There had first been a happy couple here on Motu Moemoea. Now it was a happy trio.

It was clear that nothing much more was going to get done that day. No matter. What was left undone one day could always be done the next.

Chapter Forty-Three

Mélodie duly installed herself in the treehouse.

Alexandria pressed her to sleep in the main house, where there were comfortable spare rooms. But Mélodie rather fancied the treehouse. In fact, she was delighted with it. Her father was able to give her a few tips on how best to organise things, how to make the most of the beach hut on the north shore too. As a former resident of the area himself, he could give her a wealth of good advice.

Mélodie had brought all her painting materials with her. She planned to take full advantage of her visit to an idyllic tropical island to paint as much as possible. She had in mind painting landscapes, seascapes, as well as the local flora and fauna. Who knew? The chances were that some of her Nature paintings could be used, copied, for publication in her father's research paper.

They all three of them seemed to know instinctively how to respect the others' space.

Most of the daytimes they spent apart, just coming together at mealtimes, for lunch and a fairly late dinner, always finishing in the dark.

Just sometimes, early afternoon, Mélodie would stay on to help clear away the lunchtime pots and then linger a while. She knew that Alexandria did not work much in the afternoons, so did not think it too much of an invasion to hang around on some days. Needless to say, Alexandria more than welcomed it.

It was a way for them to get to know each other better.

It could be a tricky relationship. How many sons resented the presence of their mother's new boyfriend? And vice versa. It could become a real problem, enough to jeopardise the whole future of a new relationship. Something similar could happen here. A grown-up daughter, having completed her formal education and with no pressing need to work immediately, had the opportunity to visit a father who was equally not too nailed down, such that they could easily spend a whole year together.

She would be looking forward to it with special glee, only for said daughter to discover suddenly that said father was spoken for, worse than that, had taken up with a crusty old Englishwoman. Not the ideal scenario, certainly not the one which she had bargained for. As it was, the two ladies got on like a house on fire. At this rate, Alexandria was in serious danger of spending more time, not with the new man in her life, but with his daughter.

Mélodie, like her father, refused to take life too seriously.

She had seen at first hand and too often what happened to those who did, to those who were only too ready to buy into the system, to play its games, effectively to hand themselves over. In fact, she had to look no further than her own mother for a prime example.

She did not find it attractive, was not rushing to follow in said mother's footsteps. In truth, she had decided a long time ago that she was not going to hand herself over to anyone or to any system.

No, if anything, she preferred the free spirit example set by her father. Okay, he in contrast was not exactly rolling in it, counting his wealth only in terms of shirts and moccasins. But he was free somehow, probably freer than anyone else she knew.

Since taking his sabbatical from the University of Lyon, he had also become probably the most contented person she knew. Now, seeing him together with Alexandria, a couple seemingly made for each other, he probably was the happiest person she had ever known.

The ironies were not lost on her.

What did they say in the west? - Stick with the winners! Well, she had news for the west, that is, if it had the capacity to understand, to appreciate irony and see a deeper truth. Mélodie had a new piece of advice - Stick with the losers!

She knew full well how they would all be labelled by the west

- especially her father and his new lady friend. It really was amusing enough to make one laugh. No, she had made her mind up - she would stick with the losers and thus prosper. It could not fail.

In time it was interesting to listen to Mélodie's further thoughts, her new ones.

"I can really understand now, Papa, how you found contentment out here, first in the region, on the main island, then out here on Motu Moemoea, even before you fell in love with Alexandria. I'm feeling much the same. Just now I have this daily contentment, not wishing to be anywhere else."

Julien was listening intently, just as if it were Alexandria. Mélodie continued.

"No, of course, I'm not planning to stay on here for ever, I mean remain permanently unattached. Like you two, I would like to give love a chance and for that I would have to return to the outside world, whether it be in the Pacific or back in Europe. But it's funny - how unattractive that last option now feels. It's as if the whole of me sort of rebels against the idea. Nor am I certain that it will change in time."

She drew another breath.

"I say that, not even having known the worst of it. University almost by definition is an artificial little world, in which you are at least fifty percent protected, maybe more. But even from within that security, I saw enough - to make me not want to make any sort of permanent home, either in the land of my birth or in that whole continent. I mean to say - life there is just becoming less and less natural. Being out here now, I can see so clearly. But above all it is my feelings which are aroused. Just now they seem to be screaming at me - 'Wherever you go, whatever you do, please for our sake make it somewhere where there is a modicum of naturalness left!' "

Julien was smiling. He was also nodding.

She could have been speaking for all of them.

They had each of them travelled such different routes. So it often was in life. Each had their own history, unique. Even individuals who eventually found common ground, ending up on a similar path, most often began from very different starting points and travelled very different roads to get there.

What had they in common, the three of them? Or to put it a slightly different way - in another life could they have met and been and stayed perfect strangers? Their backgrounds were different. Their characters were different. The ways that they had lived their lives hitherto were different. Even their ages were very different. And yet now they found, perhaps strangely, this commonality, this unity of purpose, almost this common mind, this common mentality.

Chapter Forty-Four

One's starting point was not generally a choice.

The road one travelled could appear to be but be less of one in practice. Even one's finishing point could be less than one hundred percent in one's control. But one learned in life. Or at least, one could learn if one were so disposed.

Even Mélodie, only now embarking on her adult life proper, might have learnt already more than many learned in a lifetime. Her father had been much older when he decided what he wanted in life, or rather what he did not want. And Alexandria had arguably waited even longer.

But it was not a race. It was not a competition. But, strangely enough, there were winners and losers. Or rather, some found more enlightenment than others. Maybe it depended partially on how earnestly they were searching. Maybe even there was about it a streak of good fortune. Or destiny. It was hard to say. Even the participants could only hazard a guess.

In a sense it did not matter. Understanding was always welcome but not always essential. Intelligence was always useful, especially if one knew how to use it properly. But in the end it was the heart which counted, the size of it, the warmth of it. That was what they were discovering now, whether consciously or otherwise.

It was about getting a feel for life.

Increasingly, society, for those growing up in it, was proving to be an inadequate school, a disappointing teacher. Arguably it was teaching the wrong lessons, getting its emphases wrong, almost misguiding its pupils when its duty was to guide them and to show them the way. But increasingly it seemed to be showing them the wrong way.

It could take a perceptive mind to realise it. It could take a strong character to resist it. And then it could take a courageous heart to depart from it, to take a different path.

Perhaps it was that which united them, this disparate threesome. Somehow, arguably against the odds, they had found within themselves some of those fast disappearing qualities. Then they had believed in them, trusted them. In the end they had encouraged each other.

It should be easy to say that that was what we were there for - to encourage each other. But how often was that encouragement missing from our circles - of family, of friends, of colleagues? How much more often did one find there only dull, unimaginative advice - to be prudent, to be safety-first? How often did that in truth, for a number of motives, some dubious, turn into positive discouragement?

But they, the three, somehow had found the other way. And it worked, worked well. That was why they could, all three of them, now wake up each morning with a joy in their hearts, one which lasted all day, one which would unfailingly be renewed the following morning.

One evening, finishing dinner in the dark, having watched the most gorgeous sunset sink beneath the waves and all three of them having drunk a goodly amount of beautiful red wine, they were all feeling warm and merry.

"May I propose a toast?" asked Alexandria.

There was no opposition.

"Here's to Motu Moemoea, renamed by me 'Îlot des Rêves Brisés'. I didn't know at the time what that would come to mean. I knew that I was bringing my broken dreams with me. I think that I expected to live amongst them, for them to be my daily companions, living out a rather sad life, but the only one possible. In truth I did bring them with me, only unexpectedly to bury them here, deep in the ground, sort of freeing myself, allowing myself to open up to life again. I guess that I will always continue to believe

\- in the universe."

She paused to take a sip of wine, as if needing to compose herself. Nevertheless, two tears ran down her cheeks, Yes, she really was, in her own words, just a sentimental old fool.

"But little did I know that the universe was going to send me another dream, not a broken one this time but one gloriously intact, in the form of a lovely man, your father, Mélodie. He has filled my heart as no man was able to do in the past. He has taught me how to live and love, to give and receive, in the way that we are designed to do. So I thank you and bless you, universe. No, I'm not going to change the name of the island back to the original 'Îlot des Rêves'. There's no need. Plus, I don't want to. I still consider the name appropriate, even today. For me it will always be the Islet of Broken Dreams, the place to which I brought them and buried them and then found real love, real life. Here's to Motu Moemoea!"

Julien and Mélodie both echoed her.

"To Motu Moemoea! To real love! To real life!"

They all drank.

They all embraced. They drank again. They all embraced again. They drank some more. At this rate they would still be toasting at midnight.

But the mood was happy, as it should be. The prospects were good. It seemed almost impossible that they would not, the three of them, spend a wonderful time together during the coming months.

Beyond that, no-one could now. No-one needed to know. All one needed to remember was that belief should always be kept alive. Yes, sadly, in the world there were broken dreams. But, less sadly, you could bury them. And then, even better, find a new and beautiful one.

The End

David Stuart Robinson

Islet of Broken Dreams

Other titles by David Stuart Robinson –

Stand Up the Real

The Archduke has been Assassinated

Journal of a Jezebel

When the War was Over - parts I & II

Trio in F Sharp Minor

The Adventures of Clarence the Duck

Alfie the Naughty Bunny

Islet of Broken Dreams

About the Author

David Stuart Robinson attended Manchester Grammar School and Cambridge University. He worked in overseas insurance and IT but now earns a crust as private language tutor. He has done conservation work and has taught abroad. Traveller, music lover, enthusiast for the outdoors, a few years ago he left the UK, first for France then for southern Spain. Like many of his main characters he is driven by passion and is always searching for greater freedom. 'I am more interested in exploring our inner life than our outer life.'

Islet of Broken Dreams

David Stuart Robinson

Printed in Poland
by Amazon Fulfillment
Poland Sp. z o.o., Wrocław